SMACKED
& other stories of addiction

Dominique Hecq grew up in the French-speaking part of Belgium. She now lives in Melbourne. She writes across genres and sometimes across tongues. Her works include a novel, five collections of short stories and twelve books of poetry. *Kaosmos* (2020), *Tracks* (2020) and *Songlines* (2021) are her latest poetry offerings. With Eugen Bacon, she also co-authored *Speculate* (2021), a collection of microlit. Among other honours, Dominique is the recipient of The Melbourne Fringe Festival Award for Outstanding Writing and Performance (1998), The New England Review Prize for Poetry (2004), The Martha Richardson Medal for Poetry (2006), the inaugural AALITRA Prize for Literary Translation from Spanish into English (2014) and the 2018 International Best Poets Prize administered by the International Poetry Translation and Research Centre in conjunction with the International Academy of Arts and Letters.

Spineless Wonders

PO Box 220 STRAWBERRY HILLS

New South Wales, Australia, 2012

www.shortaustralianstories.com.au

First published by Spineless Wonders 2022

Text © Dominique Hecq 2021

Cover design by Bettina Kaiser

Typesetting by Camilla Cripps

Editorial assistance by Olivia Ioanides. Publishing assistance by Abby Hugman

Publisher Bronwyn Mehan

Typeset in Garamond Pro

Printed and bound by SOS Media

ISBN: 9781925052732 (pbk)

A catalogue record for this book is available from the National Library of Australia

SMACKED
& other stories of addiction

Dominique Hecq

This project has been assisted by the Copyright Agency's Cultural Fund.

To Eugen and Julia

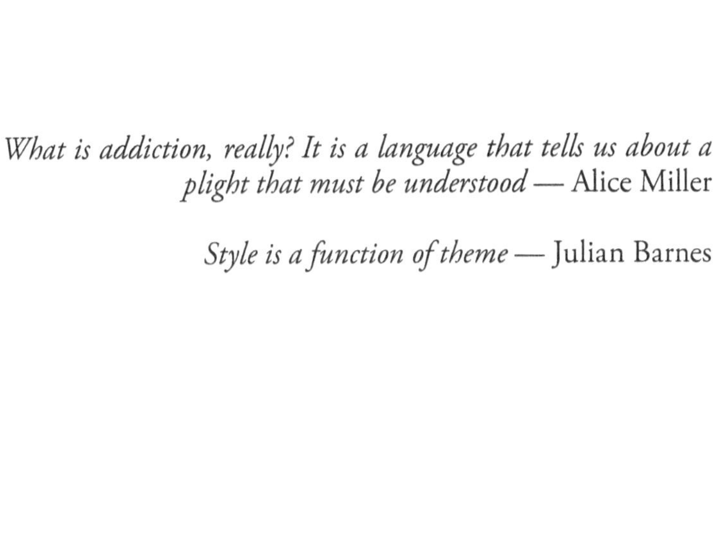

What is addiction, really? It is a language that tells us about a plight that must be understood — Alice Miller

Style is a function of theme — Julian Barnes

Contents

Preface

A portal to addicere

In *Smacked and other stories of addiction,* Dominique Hecq immerses the reader in a torrent of released waters, a ticky-tacky-tock of anticlockwise tickers in subtle yet potent stories. The assemblage is a topography of the (im)possible in new and deep-rooted fictions that are not wrath or melancholy, just anomalies.

In crafty stories that are evocatively different and covering gems such as 'Beyond the Doubting of Shadows', with its imperceptible yet too discernible events, 'Stone Heart', with its deconstructed multiplicities, and 'The Perfect Bloody Mary', with its shame and nonshame in the everyday, what do café girls, wandering lovers, aloof students, absent mothers, heart worn professors, misplaced siblings, unclued tourists, retired villagers or unacquainting fathers have in common?

Fixation.

As the sea sweeps a forlorn shore, the dusk falls across a deep quiet, and an ibis soars over a serrated crag, Hecq offers more than a taste—it's the deepest caution swathed in gentle viciousness that is deceptively tranquil inside tempest text.

Addiction is a friend or a memory, a mismatch or a trick. It's a moon of many faces refracting all you know, until it doesn't. It's unassuming camouflage, junked-up love.

Addiction is not alien, accented. It's familiar. A multi-voiced nymphette full of intent. She switches faces, mirrors, walls. Photographs, scans, refocuses your obsessions.

Addiction is a melt in array, a count with dampened eyes. He murmurs ruminations about saints and sinners, moves time until it passes. Textures you in monochrome.

Addiction comes in rainbow, unrainbow. It is a never-ending spasm, crush, quake … It fragments you, zooms you to phantastic places that locate your realism.

Addiction is a gaze. A certainty that drifts without iniquity. It slips unnoticed, then overcomes. It is a rush, tidal. Dog eat dog, a carnivore thinking it's an omnivore as fur thrusts down its gullet, the trail of torment along its innards no more than exquisite extravagance.

As your distinctions haze between a concert hall and a mausoleum, and your muscles ripple, your postures (re)arrange themselves in the arms of a ponytailed man inside a dance studio radiating sex, a faraway croon echoes closer to your ear until the lingering murmur is a never-ending dreamscape: You love me. You love me not.

Hecq writes playfully and with irony, thrumming prose and poetry in self-aware stories gravid with familiar yet unfamiliar protagonists and their dented victims or saviours. *Smacked and other stories of addiction* is a tight-rope of connections and metaphors, the reader walking on tiptoe with a balancing pole, yet at the same time craving a haircut or a quince.

—Eugen Bacon, author of *Claiming T-Mo* and *The Road to Woop Woop & Other Stories*

Just a Taste

Addiction (n.)

1. c. 1600, tendency, inclination, penchant (a less severe sense now obsolete); 1640s, as state of being (self)-addicted to a habit, pursuit, etc., from the Latin *addictionem* (nominative *addictio*) an awarding, a delivering up, a noun of action from the past participle stem of *addicere* meaning to deliver, award; devote, consecrate, sacrifice

e. g. A writer whose addiction was grant applications. Now mere fabulations. See addict (v.). In the sense of compulsion and need to take a drug as a result of prior use of it, from 1906, in reference to opium (there is an isolated instance from 1779 with reference to tobacco).

Addict (v.)

1. 1530s, (implied in addicted) to devote or give up (oneself) to a habit or occupation, from the Latin *addictus*, past participle of *addicere* meaning to deliver, award, yield; make over, sell, properly give one's assent to, figuratively to devote, consecrate; sacrifice, sell out, betray, abandon, from *ad* / to + dicere, which means to say,

declare, from the Proto Indo European root *deik-* / to show, also pronounce solemnly and akin to adjudge, allot.

2. Related to addiction and *addict* are the terms *addicted,* not as serious as addict, perhaps; and *addicting,* whose full ambiguous and ambivalent force falls on the person of the addict. Think of it.

e. g. A book about the idea of being addicted or devoted to a substance or practice.

Last Leg

W lay still. She watched the new day seep into her room, drifting, all the way down the wall and across the floor. She was sure she wouldn't live through it.

The woman who came to be known as W lived in a block of bedsits, a tenement in one of the inner suburbs of Melbourne. W was of a dieable age. She could have been thirty or forty something. She could have been slightly younger. Or older. Her body was wiry. Taut. She looked spartan. Spare. Perhaps this is why people avoided her.

W was from Wales. She had lived most of her life in rented rooms in Llangynidr, then Cardiff, but mainly London, where she earnt a living as a nanny from the age of sixteen. She was known as Wallis, then.

W saw a tenement in the city of Yarra as an anomaly. A luxury, almost. She had her own space, and she could keep it for as long as she pleased. No-one knew anything about her. It suited her. After all, she had nurtured her solitude with more devotion than her body. That had not been easy, and she was proud of it.

W devoured information. The internet had been a boon, but she liked the television best. Sometimes, she could be heard through the poorly insulated walls, screaming abuse at the box. She would rage at everything: the news, advertisements, sitcoms, cartoons, soap operas, football games and pseudo documentaries. Somehow, the television aroused her loathing for humanity.

It wasn't that W hated people. She was, after all, herself, human. Or she usually saw herself as such. But an incurable addiction to the fast pace of life and the amputation of a limb meant that she often had her doubts. She had succumbed to a desire she little understood. Now, she shunned people. She knew people and so had chosen to banish herself from their company.

W found the tenement convenient for reasons she would have liked to see as secret. There was, of course, no shortage of speed. An elderly Kazakhstani couple two doors down from her flat imported the stuff through their son's catering business. W loathed the foreign accent and the old woman's intent way of staring at her. But she didn't really care. They were always in business and always at home.

W's habit had long since claimed her right leg, just above the knee. When she was allotted a disability pension and subsidised housing, she had decided it wasn't so bad. This is why she never thought of renouncing her British nationality, which was odd, as it made her a stranger both at home and abroad. Besides, she had a quality chair and a surprisingly efficient prosthetic leg. So, between her British pension, a meagre supplement from some long-forgotten Welsh fund, and the mixed blessing of Australian methadone, W was able to maintain her health, well, habit, but she preferred to think of it as her health.

Camouflaged in unassuming clothes from a local department store, W would melt into the urban crowd. Still, she would shudder at the memory of those few periods of withdrawal, both voluntary and otherwise. Taken unawares, she would shudder in public spaces – the Bourke Street Mall, a tram stop on Spring Street, the Treasury Gardens – and she would cringe at the averted gaze of onlookers. Despite appearances, W was an inveterate junkie.

She had lost her leg because it became gangrenous. The doctor said it was because of the drugs. He had looked disgusted, not concerned. He must have been right. W was using lots of different stuff then. Mixing it up and jamming it in. Jamming it in anywhere she thought would give her the best hit. Anywhere she could find a vein and trap it long enough to stab it. Wounds on her leg became infected. She didn't care. In fact, she hardly noticed. The leg started to die and they had to chop it off before its death caused her own.

After the surgery, W promised herself never to use the needle again. The golden handcuffs were no longer an option. She started snorting junk, smoked it and mixed it with various liquids so she could drink it. It wasn't the same. It would never be the same and she knew it. It was all she'd ever truly loved and all she'd ever be good at. It was her fantasy and her nightmare. It was difficult to think of anything that wasn't somehow related to junk. Like showing inkblots to a lepidopterist and asking him to imagine what it would look like.

She was careful when she started again. Always using fresh works, keeping her wounds clean. She had done so with success for a few years. One slipping unnoticed into the other. Like the tide, her habit fluctuated. Like the moon and its many faces, it took on different urges, suppressing darker desires.

Her body soon became tired. Her forearms scaly. Her bones a grim topography. The fingers of her right hand could no longer form a fist. It became impossible to pierce the skin, let alone raise a vein.

W was never good with her hands. But still. The impending loss of her right hand devastated her. The television lost its appeal. She pawned her computer. She visited libraries and got interested in early texts about addiction. She got stuck in the Renaissance. It was a sign, she hoped. She lived in the State Library. Read books. Made photocopies. Took notes about the escalating pace of life across centuries. She surfed the net. She even sent honey talk via email. It had the advantage of remaining anonymous:

> *Gather me balme and cooling violets,*
> *And of our holy herb nicotian*
> *And bring withall pure honey from the hive*
> *To heal the wound of my unhappy hand.*

What else could she do? It was all she knew. She tried, sometimes, to force her mind into the cracks and crevices of memory, to recall something that didn't sting like drugs or stink like death. She tried thinking of friends, but her memory played tricks. It was as if she had memories of having had memories. A mismatch of names and faces.

Then W went for the big one. Crack. She felt light. But it got messy. Here were the living. Here the dead. It was unclear where to draw the line. All the same, W made her choice. She'd rather die with handcuffs made of light than live with golden ones.

She lay still. Day after new day seeped out of the room until the stink hammered down the door to her world of light.

W was taken to the morgue. An autopsy. Half her body had been dead for a lot longer than the rest. She was refrigerated in a big stainless-steel drawer marked with the letters VVO. Wallis randomly split into some meaningless ideogram. It was the sixth drawer in a wall of seven. Nobody had much to say. In fact, no-one could be found to identify the corpse. W was cremated at the expense of the Australian taxpayer.

Rrose Selavy

Though she has two left feet, Rrose Selavy has always liked the idea of dancing properly. Now seventy-seven, she still thinks about it as she sits at the bar. It distracts her from the pain. She will never say that she is in constant pain. Not quite a partner, the stool is her favourite place. When she sits at her bar with a cigarette in one hand and a drink in the other, Rrose does not seem to have a fleeting paper existence.

Cigarettes are what Rrose calls her little death. Smoking reminds her of her former self, when fags, or ciggies, as she sometimes called them, were the necessary props of courtship rituals. She enjoys the feel of the packet in her surprisingly youthful hands, then watches with fascination the imprint of the perfect white cylinder between her index and middle fingers, the white rings of smoke rising in the air, the softening wreaths of blue, the slow dying of perfection in a soft crumble of ash. When she flicks the ash, her diamond ring flashes and she feels sexy again. Even now you could easily believe that she'd once walked down the catwalk. But it is not so much her body, nor its poise, nor even the size of her diamond, that Rrose is proud of; it is her hands and the assumed sophistication of their gesturing.

It is Rrose's mother who told her years ago that you can tell a lot about women by the state of their hands. Her mother used to say that most women have coarse hands. Rrose could hear the disdain in her mother's tone. From that time, Rrose has cared for her hands. Even now she is content enough to go out without a new outfit, shoes or handbag, but never without a fresh coat of nail polish and a slathering of hand cream.

Rrose never knew her father. She is not sure that her mother did either. Though they lived in poverty, she was not aware of it at the time. Rrose's mother had endless faith that things would work out for the best. She often talked to God about their finances and urged Him to look after them.

Rrose and her mother lived near the old port in Marseille. Every Sunday, they'd walk to the wharves to watch the exotic cargo ships coming in. She remembers staring out to the open sea, watching the boats growing bigger and more distinct by the minute. She remembers one boat in particular. A heavy sloop, low on the water line, rigged with sails, but furled in. It was moving fast, with a widening white tail curving at the back. On the deck stood a tall black man with a smile to curl up inside and sleep. The man's right arm held a woman's shoulders, her slender body waving like seaweed, her curls unfurling on the soaring rich cream skin of her bare back.

As the pain increases, Rrose finds it hard to stay put. She gets down from her stool and grabs the stick she always rests against the bar – a seventies extravagance she once thought a necessary addition to the newly opened kitchen. She paid for it herself. Slowly, she starts moving around the house. As she straightens her back, she concentrates on not hobbling, watching intently the cut diamond on the hand that guides the cork stick with the ivory handle.

Rrose pauses in the living room. It is small – much smaller than the living room at the farmhouse where we spent close to ten years together. Rrose brought with her an old armchair, once owned by her grandfather, and a midwife's chair from her great-grandmother. There are three Persian rugs on the floor. Because the landlord won't allow pictures on the wall, she bought bookshelves for three walls. Crammed with slim volumes of poetry from all over the world, these, she says, make her feel more at home. Rrose once vowed to buy the house, but her vow went up in smoke when our eldest son lost the use of his legs in a motorbike accident.

Past a bunch of flattened cardboard boxes stuffed in an orange milk crate is a lounge that opens to a dining room. Rrose seldom comes here now. The dining-room table is – or used to be – a writing and sewing and drawing table, a sorting table and a mealtime table, too. Best of all, Rrose now says, is an old piece of farm machinery: a vegetable seeder. It is an exquisite piece of rusted sculpture and it sits next to the cherry pitter among the mess on the table.

Rrose, who thought she had long given up on the details of her life, now sees that the old chair is turned towards the window, an open book straddling the right arm. It is one of her own books of poetry: *Eros c'est la vie*, much faded by the sun. The floor rugs are covered with pieces of thread and discreet piles of paper. A Paper Mate ballpoint has leaked on the rug.

Rrose walks into her bedroom, right across the hallway. On her chest of drawers is a collection of old photographs. Here she is as a younger person looking straight into you. Because her gaze makes you uncomfortable, you don't notice her strong jaw. Nor do you wish to dwell on the glossy dark ringlets, the vaporous dress hemmed with frills, the multi-stringed pearl necklace. Here she is again in the company of fellow students: a tall fellow in a chemise and wig I never knew stands behind Ramon, the one in a priest's vestments. Yes, on all fours. And there is Rrose, of course, reclining on a chaise longue – suspenders showing through her dress, cigarette smoking away in her right hand. It was the late sixties. Rrose and consorts were anti-hippie. They were interested in pranks, semiotics and psychoanalysis. They regarded themselves as living poems. Some argued that what they were doing had been done to death by the surrealists, but they scoffed at such comments.

They were the only true revolutionaries. One picture of Rrose testifies to this: here she is in a cocked hat, plain jacket with a stiff collar, waistcoat, gloves, knee breeches, boots and scabbard. Next to it, a faded colour print dating from the mid-seventies shows me wary with watchful eyes, not quite participating in the moment. Observing, as though thinking I won't be surprised when things happen.

People used to laugh at me – at my blank face. Did I know that my face was blank? I was always timid. I guess that's why my father tried to find something I was good at. I happened to be good at swimming. And so, I became a solid swimmer.

I never was what people call a problem. What I was, I never quite knew. All I know is that I didn't break out the way other women of my generation did. Though I did travel. I was predictable and I married a man who hid from me during our entire married life despite his giving me two boys. For that, I was always grateful to him. No-one was more surprised than me when I left him.

Wind slaps against the house. The shutters feel as though they are about to blow open. The window frames clatter. It is hot and stuffy inside. Rrose walks out of the bathroom, working some Hydraderm into the back of her hands. She scrambles through the hallway, and slips out of doors, past the pot plants jammed with cigarette butts, past the azaleas on both sides of the pathway to her gate. The gate creaks and slams shut behind her. There is a racket of birds in the conifer tree next door. She is oblivious of the noise, the heat, the wind.

Rrose's gait is uncertain at first, but as she gets moving down Park Street her step quickens: a few smaller steps make her left foot lead. Crossing over to where the shade is, she suddenly remembers that she has a body and a heart trouble. She resolves not to push herself too hard, taking deep breaths, aware of the sweat trickling down the small of her back.

Before she knows it, she has walked further than she had intended. Indeed, further than she had thought possible at her age. She wipes the sweat off her forehead, the bridge of her nose, and the back of her neck. She peers into the new shops on Glenferrie Road, wondering how long they have been there. How long it has been since she left her stool. She can't remember ever seeing the Pukka Tukker take-away, the Saigon Orchid Manicure Salon or the Rio Argentina Dance Studio. For a split second, she imagines herself in another country.

Rrose is in Brussels. She is seated at the terrace of a brasserie on The Grand-Place, a glass of riesling in one hand, and a cigarette in the other.

Brussels is where we found each other. I could say *again*, but Rrose had become such a different person that it wouldn't feel right. Her grey hair was cropped short. I watched her comb it with open hands. It looked like loose wire wool, enhancing her newly pinned back ears. We were like two slightly mad, mongrel dogs wondering if it was worth having another go at each other. That was nearly twenty years after our falling out and I didn't pick it that Rrose's consuming of lovers might have been a sign of despair. I assumed it was part of her new lifestyle: she had bought an antique shop and after giving up the hunt for primitive craft she specialised in Art Nouveau. She had become an expert on Victor Horta and Lalique. Had I followed her instructions then, she would have disappeared without a trace.

But we were to meet again in Paris. Rrose took up my challenge and invited me to meet her at her Marais apartment.

Just imagine: glossy grey ringlets, powdered skin, painted lips parting into a knowing smile. The works. I sense she's had a facelift – she will later confide to me that she had, to celebrate her sixtieth birthday. Despite her age, Rrose is dressed to kill. She is wearing a black brocade skirt and a fur jacket in a cropped-sleeve shape over a wispy cream blouse and snakeskin pumps worked back with opaque tights. How she manages to move so smoothly in her tight skirt and high heels must defy the laws of gravity. She leads me into her living room and opens an art folio on the table. She searches through the folio, rearranging the work in sections: sketches, decalcomanias of desire, collages like metaphorical statements, poster poems, commonplace phrases scribbled on metro tickets, poems and prose-poems. As she sifts through the work, you can see that she is assessing each piece.

Maybe, she says, these are worth shipping back to Australia with all that. She gestures towards a collection of movable objects gathered into two display cabinets. These objects, I realise with a shock, testify to the wild life Rrose was leading when I first knew her: I recognise her *Fur-covered Honey Pot*, *Spectral Gorgon*, *Suspended Balls* and *Stringed Shoes*. The rest I've never seen.

Rrose and I had met over two decades earlier outside St Denis. My eye had caught a figure hailing a taxi. The grace of it. The frenzy, too, as the figure in a dark green three-piece suit adjusted his cravat. Looked at his watch. Hailed again. For, you see, before Rrose was Rrose, Rrose was Lionel.

Born and bred in the outskirts of Marseille, Lionel later studied art in Paris. We met during this prolific period of his. I didn't know then that he was to become famous. I guess I was just going along with the flow. But Lionel sprang into notoriety with a painting inspired by me: *Structure Descending a Staircase*. Some critics praised him for being bold; others demoted him for being derivative. Followed *Lilies in Furs*, *Pleasures and Infinite Pain*, a tryptich that bemused all critics. As did *Sign*, a varnished piece of shit, *Lack*, a pink butynol penis in a state of detumescence, and *ERRecTom*, a hollowed-out toilet with a solid middle made out of laminated glass. Some critics praised what they called Lionel's anti-art to the skies. Others called him a pervert or genuine lunatic.

But Lionel couldn't care less. He was tired of the art world and had applied for an Australian visa. As it turned out, he didn't need a visa: we got married on impulse in Barcelona. By then, I was collecting lists of baby names. So, you see, in our own ways, we all carry around the world our own portable museums.

Unlike mine, both Lionel and Rrose's portable museums exclude traditions. They have to be respected for this. At least, from an artistic point of view. From a personal point of view, I'm not so sure. Rrose always made a point of telling and living the truth – crazy and destructive though that might be. Lionel, on the other hand, was a living truth with the structure of fiction. The worst for me, is that our marriage was built on a lie.

Lionel and I were ill-matched. I, for one, was too serious for him. He needed mischief and a bit of rough stuff to keep him interested. I knew this from the first time we made love.

Three o'clock in broad daylight. He'd taken me back to his apartment in *Le Marais*. He untied me. Balanced the ashtray on my left breast. The glass felt cold on my skin. The smoke of his aromatic cigarettes mingled with the metallic, musky smell of lovemaking. He brusquely asked me what my perversion was. I couldn't answer. He sighed. Cupped the ashtray aside. Got up. I closed my eyes. I could hear him rattling bottles. When I opened my eyes again, he was standing naked by the vanity table, pouring us some Chartreuse in crystal glasses. We sat up in bed and clinked glasses.

See, he said, how the green catches the light behind you?

Lionel loved staging little dramas. He liked rituals. I never knew what these were supposed to mean, but didn't mind. I thought only an eccentric would do these kinds of things: play *Battleship* hours on end against themselves, carry a basket of grapes poised on their head around the apartment, paint their toenails the colours of the rainbow. By the time we settled in Melbourne, I knew he was more than an eccentric. What I didn't know is how he was to use his Tuesdays.

At the bottom of the stairs to the Rio Argentina Studio, Rrose watches a slim, olive-skinned young man, his ponytail pulled back into a red band. He slips his arm around a young girls' shoulders and together they run up the stairs.

On her way back, Rrose notices a lime tree, its branches, twisting as though affected by arthritis, stretch over her head. She remembers how her boys used to believe the lime tree in their garden had grown from the pips they pushed into the ground. How they feared that swallowing a pip would make them grow a tree in their bellies. How they pictured it would end up poking out of their mouths. The shadows lengthen under the tree – on and on until Rrose feels too dizzy to think.

That night, Rrose tries re-reading *Eros c'est la vie*. She dozes in between poems, talking to herself about the young man as she wakes.

What about that sleaze ball going into the Dance Studio? How can any man dress like that? How can any girl bear to touch him? He's all tight pants and soft dancing shoes. No spine. No lips to mouth words with. The way he danced a slinky dance with that dish of a girl. Sex by proxy, I call it. Animal sex. Nothing erotic about that.

The next day, Rrose looks through the window of the Dance Studio. The young man with the ponytail stops beside her.

Do you like ballroom dancing?

Well, young fellow, I know my ballroom dancing, but what I see in there is nothing like I would imagine dancing to be.

Come in and watch. I bet you danced when you were young. You'd have moved well.

One Tuesday I came home early from a shift at CASUALTY. I parked the car in the driveway and let myself in through the front door. I could hear snippets of conversation over Ravel's *Spanish Rhapsody.*

She's a goose.

Course she is.

I prefer duck myself. Just imagine, Ramon, a barbecued duck. Big juicy drumsticks, golden skin that lifts from the flesh. You peel it back. Gosh, what tender breast!

Lionel had been doing the ironing. You could smell freshly washed fabric and the faint metallic odour that hangs in the air after you've ironed. I walked into the lounge. Lionel was facing me. So was Ramon. Both were seated in their chairs, legs thrust onto the table on each side of a pile of ironed clothes, the iron standing on its heel rest at the far end of the ironing table.

A cosmetic case opened in front of them next to a plastic set of *Battleship* and a pot of *Clarins* hand cream. Lionel was adjusting the red satin gown he had bought me for Christmas to his – well … plump bosom. The thought of asking him where the fishnet stockings and black pumps came from didn't cross my mind.

In a theatrical gesture, Lionel exhaled three perfect rings of smoke, put out his cigarette and rested his chin on his palm. Glared at me.

What's gotten into you?

What's gotten into *you?*

Look, said Lionel, eyes closed, as though trying to keep something in.

At what?

Let's go, said Ramon. I don't like scenes.

Rrose watches as the teacher explains to his student what the tango is about, how it is the dance of poor people. How they dance it anywhere and with anyone.

It's a make-believe dance. You don't need to make a commitment. It's fun.

Rrose shakes her head. In another life, she says, I might have enjoyed that. With the fire.

When the Dance Studio comes up for sale one month later, Rrose and I buy it before the auction. It is my tribute to her for having sold her antique shop when our eldest son lost the use of his legs.

Rrose is now back on a bar stool with her bejewelled hands, looking sexy, her nails polished just that hue of scarlet. She takes out a smoke from a long slim green package. The slim black man with a smile to curl into who frets around her gives her a light. Rrose says something to him I can't catch. He bobs his head up and down like one of those toy dogs people put on their dashboards. The music is loud – *El Choclo* (the kiss of fire) by Juan D'Arienzo.

Rrose notices I'm there. Invites me over. I sit down on the stool next to her. I open my mouth, but can't find anything to say. I shift on my seat. The slim black man plonks two green cocktails on the dinky table. We sip in silence. I want to ask Rrose if she's toying with this fellow, but don't. As I turn the glass in my hand, I notice how it filters the light, giving my hands a green tinge. I take another sip and ask Rrose if she sees herself as a true revolutionary.

She curves her mouth into a faint knowing smile. She looks right through me.

Sometimes, she says, revolution just means back to square one.

Dress Rehearsal

… there's no point in living unless you are doing something towards the future. A future, of course, in which you don't expect any part — Elizabeth Jolley

It's cold in the builders' shed. It smells of earth, dead leaves and celery. Through the slats I see no moon. On my right is a shovel. On my left, a broom and a bucket. I sit with my back straight against a bag of sand. Next to it is a pile of gravel. I pick at the scabs on my knees. Gather the folds of the dog's rug around my legs. It is studded with dry grass; chafes my skin. I don't want to sleep.

The call of blackbirds. Sunshine seeps through the cracks in the timber. I hoist my weight onto my elbows, scan the shed for spiders. A black one with a fat abdomen and golden bands on its legs is eating a fly at the centre of its web. Dust mites spiral and sparkle through silky spokes. On the floor is a wilted daisy chain. I've been practising making them; I want to wear a wreath in my hair at the school production next month. *Larded with sweet flowers* … it can't be long now before she comes, before she undoes the padlock on the other side of the door. My tights have holes in them. I pull my dress down to hide my knees.

This is not what happened. Fay lied. I don't remember pushing in front of her and stopping in my tracks. Pretending to fall off my bike. Tripping her. No, I caught up with her, grabbed the back of her bike and held on. She dragged me for twenty metres and I didn't let go. When I did, she went head over turkey. She said I was adopted, which isn't true. I am the spitting image of my mother. Same hair – golden, shoulder-length. Same grey eyes. Same cheekbones. Like her, I'm tiny. My name is Di.

I sit, listening for the click clack of heels on the stepping stones, the clickety-click of the key in the lock's cylinder, the jingle of the chain. Dirt clings to my dress. The door squeaks open.

Go and put on your uniform.

I circle the house and go in through the back door out of habit. A smell of toast, butter, cocoa. Fay's eating breakfast, singing to herself: *She's leaving home* … I whip past her. *Bye bye.* Past the wicker chairs and out into the hallway. I don't know where Dad is. *On location.* But where is that? How long for? I don't expect any answers. They like to keep us in the dark. Then startle us.

Shadows play games on the wall of my room. I've no time to spare. Undress. Shove my dress and ruined tights into the laundry basket. Pause. Get into blouse, skirt, socks, jumper. The jumper's dirty. I take it off, turn it inside out. I kick the hanger under the bed, cram my books and umbrella into my bag. Spray deodorant under my armpits. Pocket a pack of tampons. Rush to the front door; knock the dry sink from the sideboard on my way past.

Hurry up. It's *my* day and I won't have *you* make me miss *my* train, mum yells.

(…)

Your shoes.

It's okay. I'll put them on under the porch.

But she's picked up my shoes and is battering my ears with them. I shield my face from the blows. One last thump, then she's gone.

As I scuttle down the stairs, I bump into Katie and her mum. Katie's been my best friend since we *relocated* – which means we couldn't afford to live in the city anymore. I've never been allowed to go to other people's houses here. *This is a country town. Nobody needs to know* … but because Katie had glandular fever last year, I had to take all the schoolwork to her house. Katie's mum is really nice. It would be hard to label her. You'd say something like *post-hippie educated.* But she hates labels. Even their farm is everything but. She's making me a dress for the school play. A peacock-coloured dress that shimmers. It's made of shot silk. It's got a camisole top with set-in sleeves and a flouncy skirt. Perfect for Ophelia. Mum doesn't know yet. She'd be mad at me. She'd wreck everything.

Diane, says Katie's mother softly. You know you could report her?

What?

How did you get this? She dabs at my cheek with her index finger, shows me the blood on it.

Oh. The cat scratched me.

Sweetie, you don't have a cat.

I love it when she calls me Sweetie. Makes me feel like I matter. I feel bad for lying. There is a sour taste in my mouth. My cheeks are hot.

Sorry.

Not another word on the way to school.

I sit and fidget on my chair. I look through the dusty window where boys and girls scatter and gather around the schoolyard, dribbling the ball, calling out to each other, shrieking, hugging. The bell rings. Books slam shut. A stampede of feet from the classroom. I wait until all have gone. A loudspeaker jolts me into action:

DI-ANN MORE, to the principal's office, please. DI MORE. My chair falls as I leap to my feet.

I'm careful not to slam the door. But the house is quiet: Monday. There is a note on the table:

> bathroom!!!
>
> get milk
>
> vacuum lounge
>
> feed dog
>
> check on Fay (schoolwork)

A dash for the fridge. Cheesecake. She won't notice if I eat a thin slice, so (…). I vacuum the lounge, scrub the bath, wipe the hand-basin, mop the floor, clean the toilet, feed the dog and then exit the house through the back door, making sure I don't lock myself out. Fay's at river dance and mum won't be home for ages.

On my way back from the General Store I linger in the uncut grass in the hollow on the side of the road, pick daisies and make a chain. I'm pleased with the result: no stems broken, no petals missing. I tie it into a bow, pocket the finished chain and set off home, quickening my pace.

Holy shit. Mum is waiting at the top of the stairs. I figure State Cross Country finals are out of the question now. But perhaps she's also heard about the play. I feel for the butterflied daisies in my pocket.

Hand-basin needs another clean. Grime around the taps.

(…)

Then straight to your room.

My breath flutters. I want it to stop beating where my heart is. My feet walk me to my room.

Waves lap at the waterside. I open my door a crack. Listen harder. Fay swooshes through the hallway, bag slung over her shoulder, a large fake bow pinned to the small of her back. I cross my lips with my index finger, nod towards the source of the sound. She nods back, slips past me. *Bye bye.* I tiptoe to the lounge, peer in. Mum's lying on the floor, breathing slowly. Her eyes are shut tight. She's listening to a visualisation tape that tells her to imagine herself swelling with light. Water is everywhere. It smells of blood and putrefaction. I close the door lest the smell engulfs me. Lest the walls of my room liquefy.

The day I complete the Cross Country final, I get home late. Light rain is falling. Mum's waiting for me at the top of the stairs, her nose creased, lips like a can opener. My back stiffens.

Nobody. Nobody, you hear, needs to know what goes on in this house, she hisses.

I didn't …

You may be sixteen, but I'm still your mother.

(…)

Now, watch it.

I feel so small. Badly want to pee but follow her up the path and into the house. Sneakers squeak on the tiles behind socked feet.

I warned you, she whispers. Nods towards the lounge.

I trail behind her. Smell fresh coffee. Sweat trickles down my neck. There is chatter in my head. Chaos in my body. In the kitchen, two city women sit at the table. Four cups. Coffee in the plunger, unpoured. A platter of shortbreads, untouched. I stick a smile on my face. The woman with yellow hair gets up and bustles forward, her black dress hugging her tight.

So sorry, ladies, Di is late, says mum in the sickly-sweet voice she reserves for school teachers and strangers.

Hi, Diane. I'm Tu-anh. Her voice quavers when she speaks. You can call me Tu. And this is Charlotte. She also gets up to greet me and teeters on her high heels. I lower my eyes. Notice the mud on my sneakers and socks.

We are from Human Services and we'd like to have a chat with you. She glances around. Continues: Let's all sit down.

I do as I'm told. Feel my breath rush in and out of my nostrils. My chest heaves.

Diane, you seem …

I listen, but don't hear. Erase the frown from my brow.

Diane, I did ask you a question.

I just fell over.

Do you bruise easily?

I'm a shocker. I look at Mum from the corner of my eye. Her face is blank. Tight.

Now, you wrote a beautiful story for the English exam called *Dress Rehearsal* …

I bite my lip.

Diane, I did ask you a question.

I, err …

Diane, I can't hear you. Tu-anh offers a reassuring smile.

She's … mum interrupts.

Sorry, Daisy, I understand your concern, but we've come to hear Diane's story …

I listen, but don't listen.

I'm going to be sick, I blurt out. Sorry. The finals.

I walk to the creek, breathe in the cloying scent of jasmine creeping across the walls of new cottages – right up to attic rooms festooned with garlands of bell-like blooms. I know there are things I can't quite understand. But deep down, I know. *Now see that noble, and most sovereign reason, Like sweet bells jangled out of tune, and harsh, That unmatch'd form and feature of blown youth, Blasted with ecstasy. O woe is me …*

Suddenly, I find myself in a swamp, surrounded by nothing but sky and the dull hum of traffic from the highway on the other side of the river. I walk along the fence where the ground is dry. Lie down flat on my back. Stare into the deep blue above. My vision blurs. I look out for the sun. And there it is.

I spring to my feet. Explore the swamp, surprised at how it sucks in my heels. *Squish suck squish suck. Squish. Suck.* My legs wobble under the weight of my heart. *Larded with sweet flowers* … I cross over to the road. Walk up past the mill, the General Store. Linger in the uncut grass, pick daisies and make the longest chain I've ever made. The chill escalates in the air as the sun climbs down. Nobody will be waiting for me at the top of the stairs. I circle the house. On the patio, mum's hammock rests in its frame, one of its loops undone. The carpet beater leans against the downpipe. The door is locked.

Production day. Nerves bunch at the back of my throat. I'm about to be Ophelia in front of hundreds of people in my shimmering peacock dress and daisy wreath. But there is another buzz in the air. Whispers. I concentrate on my part.

(They kept me back with two boys after the rehearsal. They took us to a side room. Made us wait. Then called us in. I'll be vice-captain. The principal asked whether I wanted to call my parents. No need, I said.)

I've hatched a plan. I have a real role to play now.

Off Limits

Child: an existence without a biography. A shadow rapidly fading into its successor — Milan Kundera

But I have no father, the boy screamed. His shrill call for rescue turned into an inarticulate wail.

I had to act. Fast.

I threw my arms around his body in a tight hug.

He hiccupped.

That's okay, you're safe, I said.

He kicked and punched.

I gripped his wrists.

He stopped wailing.

I stroked his hair.

He looked at me with bloodshot eyes. Face blank splattered with purple. He started sobbing.

I spoke softly: Sorry, buddy. Daddy-long-legs don't bite, you know.

The boy went wild. He pushed himself free and ran outside. He made for the dunny and locked himself up.

At least, I knew he couldn't harm himself.

I followed him out and stood behind the door.

Darling, I know it must be hard, but how about we try to work things out together?

I felt so utterly a fraud. I was a fraud. A primary teacher. Hopeless at mothering. Fathering? The wrong sex. And this new kid on the block needed both.

When Javier was only three, he'd put on his fancy outfit to go to the city with his father every second Sunday afternoon. It was a magical moment of jugglers, acrobats, whip-crackers, clowns and chocolates, diabolos and devil sticks, trapeze artists reaching out for the sky, swinging through it all and reaching out for it, ice-creams and puff cakes, his father swaying high up on the tight-rope, juggling, tumbling, clowning in swirling leisure, reaching out. Javier's father's eyes shone. He stayed in the air, suspended. He was weightless. Frightened of nothing.

At five, Javier first walked the tight-rope. He was so proud; walking the rope was what his father did. They first performed together in Brunswick Street on a Sunday in August. Their show was part of the Fringe Festival. Javier watched as his father lassoed himself, threw the rope at his feet, jumped onto the tight-rope, felt for balance and spread his arms in a flurrying gesture. When his father clicked his fingers, Javier passed him a double-ended stick and a box of matches. His father lit the stick at both ends, twirled it over his head, swung it to the right, to the left. Threw it up high in the air and caught it in one hand. People clapped. He hopped off the rope, seized Javier under his armpits and lifted him up onto the rope. Javier walked the rope all the way, a little hesitant, but beaming. People clapped. Now was the time to hop off and pass the hat around for coins.

At eight, Javier and his mother went to Ballarat. The Base Hospital, to be precise. Javier entered the ward. Saw his father plastered and bandaged on what looked like a torture rack, not a bed. He sensed his would be a tough living.

Fire sticks, our burning desires, Javier's father said – and then there's the rope.

As though holding on to a cloud swing, the son peered into his father's face. It was clueless. Lifeless.

Javier's mother told him to say goodbye and gently led him out. She later explained that the rope had snapped as his father cracked the whip high up on the rope at the Spring Lake Pageant.

You know, his mother said, Javier means bright in Arabic. It also means new house owner in Spanish.

Javier was rich with two meanings to his name, but now he had no father. He moved with his mother to a little country town about seventy miles west from Melbourne. It was a white-painted Federation style house with attic dormers and French windows flung open onto a wilderness of a garden running down to an artificial lake. It smelled and harboured hundreds of mosquitoes.

Javier's mother moved with ease onto the main street of this little town in Spa Country. People said she looked elegant and soon Javier lost track of her. Ebony hair swung about her Madonna face. She stomped in fierce harmony. That was part of the spell.

But you couldn't wave a magic wand over the world just like that.

The spell turned nasty when Javier started to think in images. Javier peeped in, peered round at his mother's parties, rooms full of smoke and spirits. The images stuck. Images of his mother flurrying him into her bedroom, hushing his mouth with a story read in haste. Leaving. Images of his mother fussing about at school functions. The Brothers praising her pluck. The priest loathing her very own living, looking on. Then there was the image of the tattoo on his arm. A sailor's knot. Javier was stuck.

Javier took action by default. One night his mother was entertaining. The lawyer of the town was drunk when he leant into her eyes and down her breasts. Said he was leaving for Europe, or maybe LA. When was not clear. When freedom calls and the time is ripe, Javier heard him say. On the dance floor, the lawyer took Javier's mother by her wrists. He led her off the verandah through the newly planted garden to the boating-shed by the lake where they sated each other in shadows. Javier eavesdropped.

Is it worth it? She asked.

How silly.

There were many in town who enjoyed the blatant efforts of a single mother to settle in respectable society. Many who enjoyed the crumbling of an honourable family, too.

Respectable folk whispered. Children sniggered at school. There were whispers in the staff room. Colourful tales about Javier's origins. His clown of a father who walked the rope. His fallen woman of a mother. People smirked. The lawyer's affair became a juicy story at The Builders' Arms. An aura of spirits hovered about him more than ever before. Children sneaked upon Javier. From the safety of ditches abandoned to dykes and piss-artists, they threw stones at his mother.

Javier's mother began to look haunted and thin. She screamed at him. Screamed at the lawyer. Beat him with her fists.

Javier went silent.

The lawyer of a lover laughed. Called her suburban, self-righteous, the nagging spider from nowhere. She screamed.

Javier gathered up his teddies and shoved them in a plastic bag. He crouched on the floor in the corner of his bedroom with his hands slammed on his ears until the screaming stopped.

At the start of the summer holidays, Javier and his mother came home early. Before them stood the lawyer, one hand on a glass, the other across a petite woman in red.

Javier's mother said nothing. She pushed him ever so gently into the kitchen, made him a hot Milo and toasted him two crumpets, spread them with butter, gave him a smile. She asked if he had any homework. Javier shook his head. He took the crumpets up to his room. Asked if she could bring the Milo.

Eating slowly, Javier looked through the window. He saw his mother walking down to the lake, staring at the surface of the water. Something in her demeanour reminded him of his father.

The next day the lawyer funded a flat in Melbourne for Javier and his mother. A refurbished first floor terrace in Brunswick Street.

And now at fourteen, Javier struggles through red eyes. To be!

He pushes me away. Kicks. Yells. He says he wants to drop out. He wants to take revenge. He knows as well as you do that tight ropes don't snap and that barmaids get hooked. He knows too that when the rush of ecstasy fades you hit rock bottom. He has struggled himself not to hit again.

The first taste was the best, said Javier's mother.

She worked at a pub – city end of Brunswick Street. She'd pass on the stuff from wealthy patrons. She paid a baby-sitter to look after her son. She told the lawyer to keep off.

Nagging spider, we're hooked, he laughed.

Get on with your life, she said.

But after her shift, at her place, they'd often drink and love wildly. Then one day she showed him. They shared. It didn't feel like a big deal. They took off.

Almost one year later to the day, the lawyer picked Javier's mother up from the floor and drove her to St Vincent's. She was not admitted. The lawyer collected her a few hours later. He screamed at her and slapped her face. She cried. His hands shook at the wheel. She sweated and wriggled. He dumped her in front of her flat.

She squatted outside, too shamed to face her son.

She walked into the night. She hunted for money. She thought that hitting rock bottom meant she'd come up again. She didn't. She picked a man's pocket on the tram and stole a cheque book and credit card. She wiped off the name with brake fluid.

Javier's mother ensconced herself in the flat her lawyer of a lover was no longer paying for. She delivered stuff and gave sex for drugs, or money. She pawned the family jewels.

One night she sat in front of a fire with a cult leader she'd shacked up with the night before. The cult leader promised she'd fade into white-oblivion. He gave her a massage. When she woke up, she undid her bonds, pushed past the curtain thrown over the frame of her bed, and screamed filth to the mock guru.

The next night Javier watched as after a hit his mother slumped onto the couch and stopped breathing. The last time he could remember, she pounded and thumped on the lawyer's chest and sat up like a zombie and vomited through her thin lips. This time she'd faded from purple to grey. Javier shook her. Slowly, she moved again.

Javier and his mother moved out. Out to a small housing commission flat. Javier's mother cut her hair short and started work in an organic fruit shop. In the evening she and Javier would watch movies. On Sundays they'd drive to the hills. They'd walk through rose farms and nurseries. Once in a while, they'd catch the tram to the Botanical Gardens. They dropped out of sight and a couple of years passed.

Next of kin?

I'm her son, Javier said, pointing at the door to the casualty ward.

Your mother's had a stroke. We need to keep her for a while before you can see her. Good night.

Outside St Vincent's it's already cold at dusk. Trees in the grey city strip shed their possums with a thud. Javier stands under a tree. Lights a cigarette and lets the wind take the smoke. His hands are shaking.

Javier can't be fobbed. He knows the lure of drugs, the look of addiction. He knows the smell of death, too. Resists the urge to call his psy.

Not that long ago his mother looked at him with sunken eyes, drooling on herself, handing him a clear wrinkled plastic pouch. His body twitched in disgust. As he reached out for it, he felt a thrill. The excitement whirled through his guts and as he opened the pouch a sudden desire to urinate came over him. He couldn't make sense of it.

He took out a crusty cream pill. Placed it on the saucer his mother used to this effect. He took a cigarette out of the packet on the coffee table. He disassembled it, extracting the tobacco with care. The silver foil tube with a spoon-like shape on the end, ready for use, he slid the end of the tube into the cigarette cylinder. He crushed the pill, placed it into the spoon, lowered the flame from his lighter and heated the fix. A wisp of blue smoke flowed up the paper tube. As he inhaled, it all surged down his throat. His body stopped shaking as he exhaled. A wash came over him like the lapping sensation of a spa pool. His pulse sped up. The tension slid away. A glaze settled over his eyes. Trails of pink and amber streamed from objects. Lights. His mother.

She came over and lay down next to him, resting her body diagonally across him for comfort. Javier enjoyed the wash of euphoria till it drained away. Down. Passed his knees. Vanished. He hoped for a return rush. Nothing. He began to sweat. He got agitated, his jaw and bones tense. Eyelids hurting. He tried to roll over. Pushed his mother away. She groaned. His hands were shaking, throbbing. Feet felt too big for his Blundstones. Lungs too large for his ribcage.

Javier waited for things to pop. Nothing. He felt like biting something. Or someone. Feel the pain pass to the victim. The perpetrator. He slammed his fist on his mother's back. She curled up. He screamed.

Shortly before midnight, Javier pounded his fists on the door of my terrace. As I opened the door, he slammed his fist into the flywire. Blood seeped out as if it had reached the point of exhaustion.

Javier wailed. Not from this fresh wound. He wailed like a newborn. He looked pale. Haggard. His bloodshot eyes unable to focus. His mouth unable to open past a grimace.

Suddenly, he burst into speech – a double voiced dialogue: one shrill voice, the other low, one whingeing, the other aggressive.

But I want to keep it.

You bitch, of course you won't. Serves you right.

Please.

You wouldn't get rid of it, you slut. Now you give it away.

Please, I want it.

We'll have it adopted out.

I'd rather die.

Pull yourself together and give me a fag.

Javier stared at me, eyes vacant, not expectant.

I was stunned. What was that? I thought of a fight over some unwanted baby. Could it be that Javier had just remembered something? Incredible though it seemed, it did make sense. I noticed a daddy-long-legs lazily making its way across the flywire.

On impulse I grabbed it and put it on Javier's hand. He looked at it.

Is that all? He asked.

That's all. Javier, I'm sorry. Take it easy.

Writing's not really my thing, Javier writes. *Mother never gave me a home. She fought for it, though. She fought for me. But she left too much out for a father. It all turned ugly when he died. It's funny I snapped when she carked it. Now there's this woman teacher – call her foster mother – handing me tea and biscuits, fussing about me. Maureen. She gave me a scrapbook to sort things out. Feels cosy on the couch. I'd like to say something meaningful. Tell her I'm joining the circus. I'll get all sinew and muscle. I'll be flyer, conqueror of ropes, predator of air, master of me.*

The Gleaners

Kay Millet crosses the bridge over the Merri Creek and pulls into Comas Grove. She parks in front of the new block of units on the left, grabs the basketful of quinces on the passenger seat and pushes the door open. Number 12 is a small sterile-looking unit, with pre-cast concrete, fixed aluminium windows, concreted front yard, no steps, no porch and no threshold. A sign by the door says: Please press doorbell HARD.

She does.

Come in, she hears, halfway through the door. She knows that Joyce will have watched her walk up the path. That she will be waiting in her chair in the front room, probably knitting, with odd china bowls of nuts and fruit on mismatched doilies by her side.

How are you darling?

Good. Brought you some quinces.

Thanks darling. Your haircut looks lovely.

She smiles up at Kay as she did last week and the one before. Sit down and have something to eat.

Kay sits down next to Joyce, off to the side of her good ear and just close enough so that Joyce can pat her knee for emphasis when she needs to.

How's school?

Kay nods her head, her mouth full of cashews.

Now darling I wanted to discuss a few things with you. I know you want *The Gleaners*. Was there anything else?

Kay screws up her face. Sighs.

Don't be like that, darling, I just want to make sure my house is in order when I go.

Joyce speaks with no sadness. She is matter-of-fact, as if she were briefing someone to water the flowers before going on holidays. They have had this conversation before. The first time Kay said she wanted the painting that had always hung over the fireplace in the old house. She knew that Joyce loved it, and somewhere at the back of her mind was the question she would ask one day: why? It showed a group of peasant women harvesting a wheat field somewhere in France. The second time she said that she wanted the picture glorifying humble rural folk. She offended Joyce with her cultural studies speak. So, the third time she presented Joyce with her own version of the painting: Ms Millet Attends a Fitness Class, because Joyce had made fun of her for going to the gym.

Okay. Welcome to gleanarobics. We're here to work out and get fit. Grip those hand weights. Pull in those tums. Bend down. And glean, glean, glean, she'd sung out in the manner of fitness instructors, pretending she was holding a microphone.

Joyce burst into laughter and before they knew it, they were both screeching with laughter. Joyce stretched out and bent down, right hand to the floor.

Not bad for your age nana.

Not as rusty as I look, darling.

Now there is a post-it note on the painting all faded with what must be four years of waiting: for Kay.

You know, eighty-two is pretty ancient. Joyce pauses. And the other day I could barely make it to the letterbox. I just couldn't breathe.

Kay smiles. She wants to reassure Joyce but knows that you can't tell her that things will get better. She might still be supple, but her heart, lungs and mind are letting her down.

How's the new medication? Still having trouble with the puffer?

Kay is not sure she wants to listen. She's heard it so many times.

On her next visit Kay brings her photo album, a thick purple phone directory sized account of all her exploits. She hopes to cheer Joyce up. Or herself, more likely. Joyce's life these days is like videotape; each day the same story rewound and repeated, the quality deteriorating with each viewing.

Joyce sits in her best chair. Her hair is set and she keeps raising her slight hand to cup and adjust her silver curls.

How are you darling? Your haircut looks lovely. Sit down and have something to eat.

Carefully placed between the pink china bowl of chips and green bowl of apples is a small pile of colourful brochures. Kay fingers them, curious.

They're lovely aren't they darling?

What are they for? Holidays?

In a way. It wouldn't be for long, of course. They are supposed to be the best miles around.

The top brochure shows two youthful retirees staring lovingly at each other while playing golf. The one underneath, a couple eating lobster in candlelight. The one at the very bottom shows a group of four elderly women laughing in a large bubbling spa. On all of them the caption reads: Vivo Village, for the best years of your life.

Retirement villages. I thought you hated those.

Joyce used to liken retirement homes and villages to battery cages for hens, small rows of monopoly pieces, prisons for the elderly. But of course, she used to say much the same about the kind of unit she moved into after her husband left.

Why would you want to go there? Kay chews her lip.

Well, you remember Carla from next door, don't you? She and her husband moved into one just after she broke her hip and before he had his stroke. She said it was a godsend, darling. Just like a holiday. Being waited on hand and foot. Just imagine.

Kay imagines. What she can't imagine is Joyce at Vivo Village. Kay had watched Joyce scrub her home like a maniac every single week for about four years before the council home help arrived. She has trouble picturing Joyce joining in with any of the cheery faced people on the cover of the brochure. Declared clinically deaf at fifty and yet conscious of putting people out, Joyce had often chosen to stay at home rather than inconvenience them.

I know what you're thinking, darling. But you give me too much credit. It would be lovely to have someone looking after me for a change. And it's not as though I'd be there for long. I'd just be passing through.

Kay furiously chews her lip the whole way home. She calls her parents to tell them how out of character this retirement village idea of Joyce's is. But her mother tells her this is a normal progression.

Nan is giving in gracefully, Kay, can't you see? Accepting the help she needs.

Kay hangs up, annoyed at how relieved her mother sounds.

Nana's transfer was surprisingly smooth, Kay writes in her diary. *Her unit was mortgaged to pay for her entry and then rented out to help finance anything else she might need. Her furniture was sold or donated and the little bits and pieces she had gleaned over the years for her dear ones were put into storage. Everything seemed so easy. I feel flat.*

From a deep sleep, Kay sits bolt upright. Her hair is matted and damp with sweat. She looks around her room in panic. No, it is not a car alarm. It is the phone.

Yeah?

Kay only hears the muffled sound of people talking in the background.

Hello?

She hangs up. Lies down. Rolls over and back, groggy. Her eyes are wide open.

When the phone rings again, Kay knows.

Hello?

Kay, sweetie, sorry to wake you. Nan's just passed away.

Vivo Village said that nana had taken an overdose of the painkillers for her hip. The doctors said she must have saved them the entire time she had been there. A nurse said she had found her lying peacefully in bed. Nana was wearing her best silk suit. Her hair was freshly set, her make-up immaculate. She had cleared the shared pantry of her stuff, cleaned up her private fridge, laid out her will and funeral plan on her bedside table.

Kay does not like what she thinks she understands as she writes. Joyce had not wanted to be one of those news-non-news-stories old lady passes, found by unsuspecting kin one week later. To her shame, Kay feels relieved.

Kay Millet drives herself to Joyce's funeral. It takes place at the small local church – classic and elegant and dignified, just like Joyce. About two hundred people. Kay stands watching the congregation shedding tears as she walks with her family behind the coffin. She chews her lip furiously. How can they stand there when hardly anyone had ever bothered to visit or call?

Nana had died alone, feeling like a burden. *Worst of all*, Kay will write, *is that the family and the church had chosen to keep the way nana died a secret. No-one knew how miserable she had been, except me, perhaps – who had done nothing about it.*

At dinner that night, Kay picks at her food, listening to her parents chatting about Joyce. There is a lot of laughter. Joyce had so many stories and so many quirky habits. Kay excuses herself and walks out.

She sits down on the low back step of what had once been Joyce's verandah. The cold concrete feels like a slap through her black skirt.

You shouldn't beat yourself up, Cheryl says, her body casting a long shadow out into the yard. She wasn't unhappy. It was just time for her to go.

Kay nods. She stares straight ahead, unsure of what to focus on.

You of all people shouldn't feel bad about this. She adored you. You gave her so much. That's what kept her here this long. She wanted to see how her crop would turn out, as she used to say.

Kay feels a heavy weight on her shoulders. Stands. Allows herself to fall into her mother's hug.

She was not all that nice, you know. Her rules were THE RULES. When she banned sugar from her house – did you know that? Grandpa had to steal sultanas from the muesli jar. When she found out, she only bought quick cooking oats and served porridge every day for breakfast.

So, what about him? How did he die?

Oh my! He's still alive. Completely bats, but the author of many books. You take after him actually.

Where is he?

Somewhere on the edge of the West Australian wheat belt. In a nursing home.

How terrible.

I suppose you could say that, yes.

Smacked

There was a last freakish flicker of lightning. Distant headland clouds drew back. A steamy stillness took hold as the sun sank behind the horizon, leaving streaks of orange and violet in the sky. The water glittered, barely moving. Tourists paused on the promenade to look at the sunset in silence, then moved on. But on the jetty, the last fishermen packed their tackle.

Just off the prom, the evening sunlight filtered through elaborate net curtains into Dot's front room. She looked through the window. Saw two teenagers like blots on the landscape. Junkies, she said to herself and turned her back to the window.

She sat down in an armchair bulging with cushions. Around her, her bits and pieces testified to a neat life of few indulgences: a refillable calendar, Capo Di Monte clowns, soft animals with large eyes, a musical box, an empty photo frame. Face followed face on the silent TV screen, mouthing words that may or may not have been important.

Dot was at one with the world. And not without reason. Seven of the eight rooms had gone, one of them for three weeks, with just the single facing south left. Some of her regulars were back. It was always good to see them; almost like family they were. Or better. No trouble at all. It was a good little business; Dot was fond of saying. It almost ran itself. She had a good girl in Georgina. She turned up at the right time and never forgot to clean under the beds. But you never knew how long these girls would stay. Jayne could be relied on for the breakfasts.

Well, why not? She'd earnt, Dot often said, the right to put her feet up a bit. A plump hand stretched towards a box of Belgian chocolates on the little side table. Expertly, a varnished nail prised open the foil: a Manon. Always nice to start with a creamy centre. Dot's lips pursed in anticipation.

The doorbell rang.

Perhaps it was someone who would take the last single – the VACANCIES sign was still up.

Dot eased herself out of her chair and padded across to the window. She carefully pulled back the festoons of net. A man in a coat with a briefcase and a small suitcase. The suitcase looked like leather. A suit under the coat. Not an expensive one, and the trousers bagged at the knees. Rep, she said, looks alright. Of course, you could never tell with reps. This one seemed alright, though. Not flashy, dowdy even.

Dot let the curtain fall and made for the front door with the composure of one who had seven rooms already let. As she reached the hall, the doorbell rang again. She paused deliberately to adjust the Visitors' Book on its gilt table and checked her lipstick in the mirror above. Then, with a tight smile born of long practice, she half-opened the door.

Evening. Do you have a room?

A single.

That's all I need.

Not one of my better rooms. But still comfortable. 'Fully en-suite'. And tea-making facilities.

The man did not respond.

Would it just be for the one night?

Yes, please.

I charge $90. Breakfast included.

Okay.

The formalities over, she opened the door wider and extended her smile. He seemed alright, a bit unsure of himself, but that was not a bad thing. Nicely spoken. Something familiar about his voice. Had he phoned in advance?

Come on in.

He stepped inside and wiped his feet with elaborate care.

The breakfast room is downstairs. Breakfast is from seven to nine-thirty, so you can have a little sleep in if you like. Your room is number 7. Second floor.

Thanks.

Now if you'd like to sign our Visitors' Book …

Dot's smile was radiant, her eyes still watchful, as she held the pen out. The man took it and stooped over the book. He wrote in long slanting letters. Now that Dot could take a closer look at him, the man's face seemed familiar too. Receding hair, dark eyes with pouches under them, a long narrow nose. Had he stayed before? Or could she have seen him on TV? Dot's dream was to fill her hall with photos of the stars who had stayed in her house. So far, she'd only had a tennis player and two raving feminists partial to Vodka.

The man finished writing, closed the book and handed it back to Dot with an apologetic smile.

This way, please.

Dot moved sedately up the stairs, one plump, ringed hand on her bosom. She always took her time going up. The man followed her in a cowed way. He certainly didn't seem to have much get-up-and-go in him. He'd be no trouble. Halfway, Dot paused and turned back. The man's face looked up, anxious.

On business or just passing through?

Err … business.

She continued upwards.

So, you travel a lot?

Quite a lot.

He did not volunteer any more information.

They reached the second landing where a floral carpet led off to the left. Dot moved along the corridor, touching a table here, a radiator there to make sure that Georgina had dusted properly.

Here we are.

She pushed open the door of room seven, stood aside. Handed him the key.

I do hope you'll be comfortable. If there's anything you need …

Thanks.

The last Dot saw of the man before she closed the door, he was standing helplessly in the middle of the room, a puzzled expression on his face.

Dot scurried down the stairs. She felt uneasy but could not say why. There was something disturbing about this rep. Something she could not quite put her finger on.

Settled again in her armchair in the front room, her bits and pieces around her, she should have felt reassured, but didn't. This thing, whatever it was, was nagging at her mind. Her hand hovered above the box of chocolates. Paused. Withdrew. She hated anything that ruffled the placid surface of her life.

Dot eased herself out of the chair and went back into the hall. She picked up the Visitors' Book, which was still open at the current page. Holding the book closer, she studied the signature: Kenneth M. Malone.

Well, she said, a shock in her tone.

For a while, the man remained in the middle of the room, staring at the bed, the patterned doona cover, frilled pillows and valance. Then he sat down on the edge.

He shouldn't have come. There was no point. Far from helping him understand, it just showed him how little he knew. It had been an impulse to take the afternoon off from the office and come down here. Even before he set out it had started to look pointless. You couldn't lead other people's lives. On the other hand, it was something positive to do, something to dispel the cloud that hung over everything since the funeral.

It hadn't worked. This small hotel room with its riots of wallpaper flowers and chipped reproduction furniture and the smell of a recently departed smoker simply made him feel worse. It had no point of contact with his own experience, nor with anything he could have imagined.

Why on earth had he told the woman that he was here on business? It had looked like the obvious way of avoiding further discussion, but … she seemed the nosy type and he did not want to go into his motives for coming. Even if he'd been able to explain them, they'd have sounded unconvincing.

He ought to go out and get something to eat. He unpacked his toiletries, went into the tiny, tiled shower-room and washed. He left the room, locking the door behind him.

As he reached the bottom of the stairs, the woman came out of a door off the hall.

Going out for a meal?

Yes.

You know the town, of course.

I can find my way around.

She hovered there in the hall, between him and the door. She still had that meek smile of hers.

Thank you, he said, and stepped around her. She made a tiny, slightly helpless gesture, as if to lay her hand on his arm,

Have a nice night, Mr Malone.

On the doorstep, he looked back and saw her still standing there looking at him through the window of the inner door. She seemed taken aback. And Mr Malone. How had she known his name? There was something about that helpless gesture and the expression on her face that accompanied it. He glanced back by the hotel door. *Prop. Mrs Dorothy Beck.*

As he went up the street into town gulls squawked. Lights came on. You could smell and hear the sea. Yes, it was coming back, the feeling he'd had when he first came to pick up Ringo, fearing the worst. Over there, he seemed to remember an amusement arcade under construction. Now it already had a faded look under its neon sign. Teenagers, blots on its facade.

Back to the main drag, he sat in the window of an Italian restaurant, looking out at the night. Leaning on one elbow, he forked greasy pasta into his mouth, a glass of red wine on the check tablecloth in front of him. Around him, couples chittered, waiters flirted with customers, the espresso machine roared. It's no good pretending, he thought. No good retreating. You have to live with it. He put down his fork.

Could it really have been her? No, it couldn't have been. Then he saw the eyes. The eyes were the same. And the voice, despite the plummy intonation patterns.

Sitting there alone in the Italian restaurant, mouth open, he saw the unkempt dyed hair and knowing grin of a girl in her early twenties, a girl with an impulsive nature and a temper to match. He tried to reconcile this quick mental picture with the hotel and its owner. Who would have believed it possible? He now wondered what Mr Beck was like.

Dot was restless. She flicked from channel to channel on the TV. There seemed to be even more sex and violence than usual. And then drugs. She poured herself a sherry to settle her nerves. Then another. She picked up *Woman's Day* and idly turned its pages, skimming over Mouth Watering Desserts, This Week's True Romance, Summer Fashion. She didn't like this feeling. Why couldn't she settle? Deep down, she knew the answer. This unsettled her even more.

Around ten, she heard somebody come in, and went to the door of her room. The Marshalls, back from their bingo.

Good night folks, she carolled.

She looked at herself in the windowpane. Patted her tight curls into place, pursing her lips to smooth out her lipstick.

By half-past ten, she was dozing in her chair. The front door banged shut. She jolted awake. Should she bother? There was no point, she thought. Then she changed her mind, got up and ambled into the hall. It was the man from the single, halfway up the stairs.

Oh, Mr Malone.

He turned around.

Did you have a nice evening? Find somewhere nice to eat?

Yes, thank you.

He doesn't recognise me, she thought. It isn't as if I've changed that much, but he doesn't recognise me. She felt disappointed, and, at the same time, relieved. After all who was Ken Malone to her? Just a face from the past. From her daughter's past. A daughter who had been silly enough to get into bad company. And ungrateful to boot. Deb had even changed her name. Whether it was to match her new taste for crack or cover her tracks, it was not clear. What was it again? Cookie. No, Candy. Candy Rorschach or something. The sooner this Ken Malone is out of her place the better.

Ken looked down at her and thought *I should say something.* Not tonight. It's all too late and too much of a shock. He didn't want complications. Not at this time of the night.

Will you be here in the morning?

Up at the crack of dawn.

I'd like … perhaps we could have a chat.

Of course.

Good night, then.

Good night, Mr Malone. And if there's anything …

Ken passed a disturbed night, shifting his head from side to side on the frilly pillows. He had dislocated dreams in which Dot's face blended with her daughter's and each spoke the words of the other. From time to time his son was there too. He kept waking up.

Dot slept like a log. Her alarm went off. She smacked it. Snuggled down even deeper into her pillows.

Breakfast was the funereal occasion that it is in many small Victorian hotels. Guests spoke in undertones, passing toast and jam furtively as though unspeakable sins had been committed the night before. Ken sat on his own, feeling exposed and drained, wishing he had bought *The Age.*

The woman who took his order was small, middle-aged and alert. She seemed more concerned to exchange gossip than to refresh toast racks and tea pots. When Ken had done what justice he could to his plate and most of the guests had gone, she fixed him in her sights.

Was everything alright?

Yes, thanks.

Are you staying long?

Just overnight. Tell me … Ken began hesitantly. Is Mrs … the owner around?

Haven't seen her yet. Always a late riser, is Mrs Beck.

And Mr Beck?

The woman let out a little hoot. There's been no Mr Beck for as long as I can remember.

Meaning he died?

No. She became conspiratorial. He left. Don't ask me how or why, but that's when trouble began … you know, Deb and Ringo …

I see.

A distant look came into Ken's eyes. He seemed to forget where he was. Then he looked up and said:

I'd like to have a word with Mrs Beck.

And now he was coming down the stairs. Suitcase packed, and ready to leave. Ken Malone large as life, who by some weird coincidence had spent a night in her hotel. She knew what she was going to say. *You aren't by any chance related to Ringo Malone?* Or perhaps, *I used to know a Malone. You wouldn't by any chance be a relation?* But first to business.

Good morning. Did you sleep well?

Yes, thanks.

A nice day for your journey.

Yes, very.

Right, Mr Malone. That'll be ninety dollars. Do you need a receipt?

No, that's fine.

He fumbled in his trouser pocket, pulled out a dog-eared wallet and produced two fifty notes.

Just a moment. I'll get you change.

She went into her front room, closing the door behind her. From beneath the musical box, she pulled out a bundle of notes and took a ten. She noticed to her surprise that her hand was trembling.

She went back into the hall and held out the note, and, as his hand stretched out to take it, their eyes met. At that point, she knew where she stood. And who he was. In silence, the implications ramified endlessly.

He opened his mouth and closed it again. He looked at the stocky over-groomed body, the tight curls, the false smile and the crimson fingernails, and he thought no, *this can't be Candy Rorschach's mother.*

She watched him hesitating. Poor thing, she thought. No drive. No wonder his son got into drugs.

Well, she said, breaking the silence. Safe journey, Mr Malone.

Thank you. Err … about Candy, I mean Deb. I'm terribly sorry. They buried her last Monday. She didn't want you to know. But I thought …

Dorothy Beck put her hand to her mouth. She stood looking after Ken Malone as he went down the steps. He turned back once to look at her, then looked abruptly away.

Everybody Says I'm a Liar

… always a liar when she spoke of her pains and miseries — Christina Stead

The sea, in its broad jacaranda sweep, bursts on the eye with its wide beach sparkling in the dazzling light. It contracts into a channel between high ultramarine walls where it seems to escape with the thick fluidity of storm blue, indigo, cerulean, only to adjust to the hue of the high walls, like slate, a colour as yet unnamed, with the guile of a tone that strikes you with a silent horror.

Suddenly, you are listening for a heartbeat.

You feel cold. Your eyes can't focus. Your breathing is slow. Spiked. Soon the world will swoon. Soon, your voice will boom in your head. Soon, your body will play dead. Soon, you will be two.

An image returns and you squeeze it out of sight.

Momentarily, you stop breathing. You know it's her. You can smell her now. Oh, how you hate her. With her pains and miseries obliterating yours.

Hi honey. I'm back.

You open your eyes and she looks like a ghost. Feels like a ghost. It gives you the creeps. Makes you a ghost so distant from yourself you want to leave this house. This life. She is so grey and sticky and smelling of nail polish and Ponds cream and snot and something salty you know but don't want to know is cum. And you want to leave.

And in that moment you know why you can't say I any more. Be that I. Be. That. Oozing pus. That salt and cream and sweetly warm stuff you couldn't stick a name to. But sticks to you.

Honey, Nails is very sick. I'm off to the hospital early tomorrow. Hope you don't need the car.

I am dead now. Can't you see? I've been dead twelve years. Red Ps, green Ps, no Ps make no difference. Why would I need the car?

Twelve years. Or is it thirteen?

They are family friends. We are drawn to them. I don't know them well. There are three children in their family. All boys. The oldest, Querol, has long black curly hair. He freaks me out, always appearing out of the blue with a smirk on his face. But he is hardly ever around. The next, Sebastian, is my brother's age and, like older brothers do, makes me want to cry for sport. The youngest, the one they call Zero, is my little sister's age. He is soft and softly spoken, too. He has spiky blonde hair and grey eyes way too big for his face. I'd lie any time to keep him safe.

Louise, the mother, is the gossipy type. My dad used to say, all coffee, wine and chats until you cross her, and I guess that is true. I saw her throw the telephone across the room once, and it smashed into the wall, peeling the new beige paint and revealing the dark grain underneath. Nails, the father, is a plasterer. He is a solid man; outgoing and funny.

I like him, but soon sense he talks of many things he never does, promises things that never happen, and see he always has a stubby in his hand. But as Louise and my mum are often on errands together and there is no-one there my age, I often talk to him. He likes to brush my hair. And he tells me I have beautiful skin. On Wednesdays he picks me up from basketball.

Their house is familiar in its kitschy unoriginality. A suburban home with panelled walls and beige carpet. The lounge suite matches the house's interior, with a three-seater couch and a curved four-seater that spans one wall of the living room. It lengthens the room, Louise says. There is also an armchair that completes the set. No-one ever sits in it. It belongs to Nails. A prism hangs from a hook above the bay window behind one of the couches. Every time I go there, I perch on the curved couch and watch it reflecting the jade of the trees and azure of the swimming pool in the backyard.

That day after basketball …

We are moving house. We've been friends with them for four years. Barbeques, birthdays, Christmases and New Year's. Even a holiday to the Bay of Fires in Tasmania for three weeks. Binalong, I think it was. That's when everything changed. When we got home there were no more drunken parties, no more being woken up at two in the morning, no more overflowing recycle bins. We still see them. Sometimes. But Zero and I have stopped speaking.

That day after basketball, it must have been about seven or eight. He took me home.

We are moving again. Dad pulls my brother and sister and I into a dark room at our auntie's house one night and says something through uncontrolled tears about mum not loving him anymore. We are going to go to a new school, living in a house without him and perhaps catching up at weekends and during the holidays. What is not explained is that my brother and sister will live on one side of the peninsula, and I on the other until things settle as they say. It seems as if all between us and our friends is over.

It happens so quickly that I don't notice much. No-one is saying anything. Dad is gone and mum is house hunting. It will be a full year before I manage to overhear something about Louise leaving her husband. In my naivety I am excited to hear Louise's story. I point out to mum that she had not been the only one without a husband. Her smile is lame, yet she continues to wrap newspaper around glasses and cups and vases, for we are moving back to our old place.

Home is just a shell crammed with the old furniture except for what Dad took with him. It's odd, but it feels empty. I ask mum where Louise is. Why she left. Where Nails went. Whether Louise took the children with her. Then one Sunday, it strikes me that I don't want to know the story at all.

The church we attend is associated with our old primary school. We know everyone there, as we did then. We sit among friends and go out for breakfast afterwards. It is the first Sunday we have been without our father. I'm not sure why mum took us, though. Is it some kind of ritual? Is it out of guilt? Is it worse?

On entering the church, I run into a friend I haven't seen for two weeks as it has been school holidays. Before I even have the chance to say hello her mother intervenes.

Mass is about to start, I think you'd better go and sit with your mother.

I want to protest, but she jumps in again.

Go and find your seat, dear.

I walk away, confused.

I still hear her words as I make my way back to my seat.

Now sweetie, remember …

I'm not quite sure what I hear. Nor what that means, but it all upsets me and I am sure whatever she means can't be true.

That day after basketball, it must have been about seven or eight. He took me home. He must have drunk his own weight in beer. That's all I can recall.

New school, new home again, my brother and sister back on this side of the peninsula. Arriving home from school not two weeks after mum and I have moved in, I bump into a removalist in the driveway.

I stand aside at the front door to let the men carting things pass and notice that they are actually moving new furniture in. Confused, I wander inside and see a different scene altogether. Beside our grey leather lounge suite is a large brown armchair. It looks ugly and out of place and I don't want it to be there. I don't want him there. I don't want to remember.

My mum and dad didn't love each other anymore. Louise's husband had done something terrible, so she had kicked him out. All of a sudden, their kids were not allowed to play with us anymore. Then we had to change schools. It's not adding up, but Mum uses her most soothing voice to convince me it is all fine now that she has a good friend. He even calls me bud every now and again, patting me on the back.

We move again. We move to be closer to the sea so Nails can surf, but all I see is him sitting in his favourite armchair, bellowing into his mobile phone, the TV on maximum volume and mum and I retreating to the kitchen where we can perhaps at least hear ourselves unfeel.

That day after basketball, it must have been about seven or eight. He took me home. He must have drunk his own weight in beer. He looked like a pregnant woman, exhaling yeasty breath punctuated by offensive burps and he had difficulty changing gears. That's all I can recall. Except for licking a violet ice-cream clean.

Honey, are you there?

The sea is a deep and narrow channel between high ultramarine walls where it escapes with the thick fluidity of storm blue, indigo, cerulean, to adjust to violet ash between breakers.

My skin crawls with uncertainties. The walls around me collapse. A wave sweeps over me, rolling me over. I hold my breath. Listen for my heartbeat and hang on to the idea of words.

Then scream.

Zapped

Today, 31 December 2018, only a few minutes from midnight, Matt is alone, lying on his back on the black, vinyl-upholstered sofa against the far wall of the living-room.

Outside, the heat is still beating down on the brick walls, on the flat roof of the house, and despite the open window there is not a breath of air. There hasn't been a breath of air for three days now.

At Matt's feet, the dog is panting noisily. It is the only sound inside except for the occasional motorcycle in the distance that makes Matt shudder.

It's as if there's no-one, absolutely no-one, for miles around, but me, Matt and the dog. The silence is weighing us down as heavily as the heat, which is like a vice gripping your head.

It's too hot to think. I get up from my chair and walk across to the sink to get some water. I fill a jug from the tap. From where I stand, I can see the dog looking up. He pricks his ears forward. I fill up his bowl. I get two glasses and a straw for Matt. I do all this without thinking. It's been a long time since I've been able to think. When I put the dog's bowl down, he lets out a little yelp and I feel sorry for him. What would a dog like this, used to chasing chooks and killing rabbits, enjoy about the city?

Yet in a sense, even in a city such as ours, by default you are too close to nature. You know and understand so much about it that it makes you all the more acutely aware of what you don't know and don't understand or don't want to face, and because of this, you're all the more likely to explain it away to yourself in terms of the knowledge you do have. Why? You do this to make sense of the senseless.

There is a sudden clap in the air.

Eager for explanations, I instinctively think of thunder and look out the window, expecting lightning. I'm quite wrong about the causal chains connecting events. But my mind nevertheless insists on making connections, just as it insists upon metaphors as a way to getting to the truth, if not mere distraction.

The fireworks have begun.

At one minute past midnight Matt is alone, lying on his back on the black, vinyl-upholstered sofa against the far wall of the living-room. He is technically one year older. As I hurry towards the window, I notice the even sound of his breathing. He is breathing a bit laboriously because of the heat. He is asleep now, or pretends to be asleep. The dog has crept closer to him. The dog and the child have grown closer together over the past year.

Outside, the night sky is wind-blown water, ablaze with arrows and asterisks zigzagging and seesawing across my field of vision. Spectacular shell-bursts cross the whole colour spectrum as though through watered silk. The air is abuzz with head-splitting explosions and detonations. Silences are ominously brief. In this celestial battlefield, yes, I am dazzle-blind.

A thick cloud is pressing on the house.

I look at Matt. Wonder what he sees in his dreams. His dreams are his second life, I want to believe. Matt has been looking for himself for twelve months now. So have the few friends who still visit him daily with their offerings of music, compassion or pity. The dog keeps a close watch on the man-child. If you get too close to Matt, the dog's eyes grow hard and his whole body becomes tense. The hair on his back bristles slightly.

As I wrote *his dreams are his second life*, I didn't know I still wanted to believe in anything. I thought I had dismissed daydreams and the business of wanting when I stopped talking one year ago – I must have known anger and guilt ought to be kept lipped in. I can now see that all along I have secretly been waiting for answers to one question: the question of reversibility, not causality.

What if? The question is writing itself in large capital letters in my mind. I can see that I must force myself not to panic, and that it is most remiss of me to stand here like a dummy, cradling my laptop, eyes fixed to the embers zizzing and fizzing in the night sky.

Looking out the window, not really seeing, I remember the last time I felt the panic surge in my chest like this and made up the verb to zizz in order to avoid zap. When the surgeon frowned at my childish expression, I commented on the phrase leading nowhere he'd just used. It was not to get back at him. At the time I thought I was going somewhere and willed the verb to zap out of my vocabulary. Now I am here. I have been here with Matt and our dog for fifty-two weeks. It was all very well for the surgeon to say let the facts decide, but ultimately, I must ask myself – decide what?

I have a horrible feeling of having committed something far worse than an oversight. I know that what I have done or not done stems from fear, not reluctance. Not even ignorance. Since we left the hospital the question has existed, but remains unaddressed, and I have been guilty of acting with two discrepant minds – one that wants the blind to follow the blind; the other that intuitively imagines or foresees, but has no desire to face up to the facts.

The fireworks peter out in white. The sky is all purple haze.

Behind me Matt is alone, lying on his back, seeing things in his dreams. The dog skittles to my side for a pat. His black and white coat shimmers in the moonlit room. He fixes his brown eyes with pinpoint pupils straight ahead, out the window.

January 2018. Outside a car engine is revving. Shrill voices rise above the roaring of the engine. I can't make out what they're saying. Deep down, I know what is going on. They're back from their parents' country property with food and unwrapped Christmas presents, some of them useless, but it doesn't matter. The baby has just woken up. They even have a TV to carry up the stairs. And there is no parking spot in sight.

Easy, she says. You stay in the car. After all, it's only after midnight.

Shut up, he says, for despite his baby face, he is a police officer.

Suddenly motorbikes slip through. There is something spectacular about this, for the bikes are Harleys. They line up at funny angles on the opposite side of the street. The bikies take their helmets off, bend over the body of their machines and dismount.

The leader of the gang walks up to the car. Do you want to do business?

The driver of the car hops out of his vehicle. Or maybe someone hops out of the car and the driver stays inside. Then voices blow up like hand grenades.

Around the corner the Indian restaurant has just closed its doors for the night. The African choir has folded for the year. The band next door is packing up. People yell and kiss and giggle from across the street. Voices ebb and flow in flirtatious or quarrelling tones. Couples stream past, elated, tipsy or just happy. A group of hooded youths waving bottles appear out of the blue. There is a scuffle – perhaps someone provoked the gang leader. Someone intervenes.

The cloud is pressing on me. The night's embers are so close that their heat fills me with fear. Everything is so slow, and yet there's something like flashes of lightning striking the city and its suburbs like signals blazing out all over.

January 2018. The young woman and her baby on a summer's night in the city bursting with the noise of people coming home, the teenage girl twirling her ponytail as she waits for her boyfriend in the electrified summer night, the driver of the car not arguing on the street, but getting the bath ready, the Harley-Davidsons stylishly racing off, the youths sharing a last joint before going home. My son coming home. The day after. The future taking shape.

How easy it could have been, then, December 2017, only minutes from midnight, to have said, pointing at the night sky, Matt, don't go out. There's a storm coming. I could have insisted, Matt, didn't you hear the thunder? Look. The dog's hiding. I could have cajoled with an early present – oh, yes, only minutes from his eighteenth birthday, with the electric guitar standing to attention in what was then my fiction room. But I let the moment pass.

The motorbikes. The angry youths. The silence. A knock on the door. These are the facts you haven't faced up to yet. These are the events you've been trying to connect for three hundred and sixty-five days. You know there's no point, but your mind nevertheless insists on making connections.

1 January 2019. Only a few minutes after midnight, Matt is alone, lying on his back on the black, vinyl-upholstered sofa against the far wall of the living room. Outside, the heat is still beating down on the brick walls. On the flat roof of the house. Despite the open window there is not a breath of air. In this city gone electric one year ago while I was writing a story, he was strolling down the street. The motorbikes were irrelevant. No-one took any notice of the hooded youths waving bottles. He tried to help. They pushed and shoved above the revving of the engines. They blew smoke into his face. Impassive, he stood still; he could feel the chill within himself. The palms of his hands got moist with sweat. They

snatched the iPod. Demanded money. The phone. The driver of the car with the baby face put his hand into the right pocket of his trousers and felt with the tip of his fingers the pocket knife his father had given him for Christmas. The driver of the car looked away.

There was a loud clap when Matt's head hit the footpath.

The driver of the car yelled out for all to stop. But they ran off around the corner, waving their bottles. The bikers hopped on their machines and disappeared in a cloud. Silence settled back down on the street. The footpath was shining wet.

The Perfect Bloody Mary

There wasn't any shame in being with a girl like that, Adam thought as he moped in the local café. Even other blokes turned or flicked an eye when she whisked past.

The café was tacky and bright. The coffee was crap, but he couldn't go back to the Bodega where the lights made the atmosphere smoky even when there was no smoke and the coffee was worth the extra and where she worked, glowing in the permanent semi-dark. He couldn't hide there from the eyes of the others who knew.

They said to him when they found out: why d'you hang out with that slut? Her sort, they run around with everyone.

He'd said: seen you guys look at her too. All of you. And they, unflinching, had said: sure, but would we run around with her, Adam? Seriously.

He couldn't stand the shame. It made him even more ashamed to feel. He'd found the café down the road and hid there, feeling worse for hiding. Worse still when he imagined her hurt at his disappearance.

They used to go to the Bodega because they let you smoke inside all day and the rich kids and classy girls stayed away. They would look in the door and wrinkle their class noses on which their sunglasses stuck, and turn away. Blank, faceless.

The food was good and came in big serves. Even the boys couldn't finish their food and sometimes when they left, the old drunks would slide into the booth and lap up the rest. Adam wished there was some way he could give them half without being embarrassed or without them being insulted. Most of the time he wasn't even hungry, and neither were the others. They just needed a place to be other than the university which had seemed so important back in high school but was now a time waster; a great limbo-like life waster.

But he never minded going to lunch there. The dark was comforting after the glare of the street and the automatons passing through it. Even the noise seemed muted and buffered by the dark haze. Adam didn't smoke, but the second-hand haze relaxed him somehow. He inhaled deeply.

Since he'd stopped going to the Bodega, a craving had developed for the sweet tobacco his mates had rolled their cigarettes with – the smell that seemed to fill you like soup on a cold day. At the café with bitter coffee and waitresses whose skin was a sickly white, people went outside to smoke. Wafts of their joints came in through the door when it opened and closed. That smell did not comfort. It hurt the lungs.

Adam sat cold in front of the window on a barstool, gazing past his starkly white reflection. His paleness sickened him just as thoughts of her did. The whiteness and blandness of everything made him ache with a boredom on the cusp of bursting into rage. The walls, the floor, the ceiling and the curtains white; the sky, the light, the faces of the patrons and the waitresses, all so white. He longed for the dark of the Bodega, its softening pulse of glow, its amber slumber. He thought for a minute that he could go back; that he could dare. That after a while his old mates would ignore him and stop jeering. He would look past their pink faces and just stare at the plush dusk. But he couldn't go back.

The first time he had gone to the Bodega without his mates was not a busy time. It was between lunch and dinner. He had skipped his evening class. They had all been there that day for lunch and as usual he'd not said much but sat on the outer edge of the booth, watching her whisk back and forth with the orders.

She took orders from their table with an air of disgust and forced superiority, angered by their loudness and brashness and the mess they would make. Adam cringed under this manner of hers. Hoped that she thought he was different. He fantasised about her knowing he was different, about him being the only decent person at that table, one who didn't think he was better than her because of his money or colour or place at the university.

He had grown up around the boys he called his mates, but never understood them. His parents had fed him all the same closed-door prejudices theirs had. None of that nonsense had taken root in him, though it lived within him like a nauseating feeling. The boys whistled at girls who seemed to him nice-looking enough but somehow dull. Seeing them flirting with each other seemed wrong. They looked mismatched. Adam imagined them having children and talking the same sideways comments that were not meant to be heard. Only absorbed by children.

The other blokes had pretty girls and even he, Adam, had them sometimes. She was not pretty. She was amazing: part of the glowing mellow darkness but sure and solid as amber. She was really there. Alive.

That afternoon as she'd taken their orders, Adam had gazed slightly up at her face as if watching a distant sky. He had seemed unfocused. Someone had nudged him.

Aye, Adam, mate.

He had come back from his sudden absence to find everyone waiting for him to order. He did. She walked away from their table. The stares of the others were sharp and fixated on some part of her body.

They looked away. Adam felt scorn for them. His watchfulness followed her in her entirety as if she were in a capsule and he was watching that capsule. Suddenly she flicked her head and turned back, startling him into momentary confusion. He thought she'd winked at him.

He couldn't be sure. When she brought the food, she gave no indication of friendliness. Yet he was sure she had winked. He watched her closely throughout the meal until one of his companions elbowed him squarely and said loudly: You're all eyes for that bitch, aren't you?

She'd been walking right past. His first reaction was: You're full of shit. As he said it, he half regretted it and half didn't. Either way, he was just saving face. His mates had chuckled. Hunched over his plate, he'd muttered: You swine. His thoughts ran around things like *you ignorant dick stupid swine racist pig I wish you'd die in a pool of shame.*

He thought now in this new café that at the time something in him knew he should try to be pleased at what that mate of his had said because that was how it was. After all, they were studying at the university. They were quite important really and she didn't have the right to look at them and treat them in that uppity way. But he fought it then. He fought it still, feeling as much of a swine as his mate.

He had gone back later that evening. Sat alone in a different booth. He waited for her to come to serve him, trying not to watch her as she went about her business. She came over. To his own surprise, he grabbed her wrist. Pulled her down into the chair beside him.

Hey! she cried out, flopping onto the seat.

It's okay.

She stared into his eyes for a second. Waved an okay to another waiter who had looked over.

Adam felt her warmly occupying the space beside him and he felt silly. What?

I'm busy.

Adam looked around. The place was empty. No, you're not.

She shrunk back. What do you want?

His hand still curled around her wrist, he felt her flighty pulse. The skin of her wrist was almost white.

I'm sorry about this afternoon and what my mate said about you.

It's okay. I'm used to it from ignorant fucks like your friends.

She gave a pert smile, slid out of the seat, straightened her uniform, positioned her notebook in her palm and poised her pencil. Now, can I get you something?

Adam felt hurt. I really am sorry. He looked down and wanted to be gone. Look, I am sorry, he said with force. That's all I came here for. He looked towards the exit away from her, determined to never come back and started to slide out of the vinyl seat as she had done.

She stopped him with a hand on his arm and bent down. I know. Stay. Have something. She smiled. On the house, she said offhandedly. Just stay a bit.

When are you finishing tonight?

She laughed and blushed. Seven. Just before the dinner rush.

He leaned back and checked his watch. Okay. I'll have a coffee then. I'll wait. Adam was filled with a warmth that completely replaced that afternoon's shame. As she walked away to get his order the warmth expanded and expanded until he thought it would explode and seven o'clock seemed like seconds, yet hours, away.

She'd be finishing in a few hours and his mates would've already left the Bodega having done their day's worth of glancing and leering at her and maybe even imagining doing to her what he had done. He was so sorry. He was so sorry to have acted just as she would have expected one of them to and every day, he sat eating these dry sandwiches wishing he could make it up to her somehow and dreaming of taking her away or even just seeing her again so she'd know what he'd meant by it all.

When she finished, she said she needed a drink. So, Adam took her to a bar.

Don't you need to eat? He asked.

She laughed. Eventually.

She matched him drink for drink in her slight body for two good hours by the end of which he felt mellowed, leaning on their small round table with the musicians blaring their jazz. She sang along to the old standard songs in a low voice that sometimes went out of tune.

They didn't talk much. He watched her. She glanced at him every song or so. Smiled over her glass. The perfect Bloody Mary, she said. And I would know: a handful of ice, 125ml tomato juice, 50ml vodka, 1 tbsp lemon juice and 25ml sweet sherry. Shake. then add a smidge of Worcestershire sauce, a drop of chilli sauce and a pinch each of salt, black pepper, celery salt and fennel seeds. Shake hard. Strain into a tall glass with ice and garnish with a celery stick, lemon wedge and a cherry tomato. She laughed. What are you, he asked silently over and over like it was the most important question that had ever occurred to him.

Eleven-thirty. Band on its closing number. The singer went out. The saxophonist rocked madly. The guitarists smiled sheepishly in the background. She and Adam were both skint by then. Her smiles were wide and easy, her lips red. He drew his chair close to her and pulled her towards him with one arm and wound it all the way around her soft small waist and she laughed and her lips drew back and parted.

You're so beautiful, he said. Tried a kiss.

She drew back. Let's go to my place.

Six flights of stairs. Her shoes clacked on the concrete as they climbed. Three flights up, she stopped. He walked into her back. She giggled. These damn shoes, she said and took them off. Resumed the climb, silent and light now bouncing from step to step with her shoes in her hand.

She opened the door. Flicked the light on and all the bottles on the floor made him wonder why she hadn't fallen going up or down those stairs yet. She dropped her bag and shoes. Stretched her back. The next thing Adam knew, he had reached around her and flicked the light off.

She was laughing through his kisses, clutching the front of his shirt and the lapels of his jacket, stumbling backwards, kicking bottles, sending them spinning and clattering until the backs of her knees touched the mattress and they both fell onto it. She looked up at him in drunk wonder.

What are you?

What do you mean? Where are you from? Does it matter?

No. No. You're still …

What?

Beautiful, despite …

What?

It doesn't matter I'm sorry.

Her skin, so pale in the streetlight, was like cream. Not with that hint of pink of his daytime mates but with an undertone of something darker.

She watched him with her large almond eyes and dark mouth made darker by the wine she was now drinking from a bottle beside her bed. She stopped drinking, her mouth breathing slow and heavy and loud breaths, her hands clutching his back. The cold in the air and their sweat spread like a thin film of ice on their skins.

Adam realised he was hurting her. When he kissed her face, it was wet. He kissed her face and she stopped crying. She placed her cold hands on his face and shoulders and chest, gasping, feebly pushing him away.

He took her hands and pinned them to the mattress with his own. He licked her face clean of tears, pushed his arms under her, lifted her body to him and buried his face in her cream-coloured shoulder, crying himself as he finished.

Sitting in the café, Adam always thought of this. How she would be working at the Bodega, serving his old mates maybe, wondering at why he never came back. He thought of it over and over and wished he had left it as it was before he'd felt that strange rage. He prayed that she understood. That she understood his sadness, too.

He wondered if he was the first or the only one who had been captivated by her in that large-serve place where you could smoke inside if you liked, and the air smelled like warm wood infused with tobacco and the lights were kept low. He would sit there and long to inhale the comforting smoke. He would wonder if anyone else like him went there to hide and drink the good coffee she made at the hissing machine and watch her twist between the tables and chairs in those shoes and deal with the loud booth of white university lads minus one that arrived every weekday lunch with stares pointed at her butt and her legs in those heels.

Adam felt old. He felt he had let ignorance and hatred own him. He feared there was no redemption. Would he ever be capable of watching anything with innocent wonder?

He drove to her building at around ten. Parked. Climbed the stairs. At eleven he heard the sound of high heels on concrete echoing up the stairwell. His heart began to thud into his chest. The clicking stopped. He heard her breathing. She appeared at the top of the stairs. He clambered to his feet. She stopped in shock. Closed her wine purple mouth. Walked up to him barefoot, shoes in hand.

I came to see you, he said.

What for?

I don't know.

She sighed. Looked away. Pushed her key into the door. He noticed the number was missing but its outline was there. She turned the key and shoved. He heard bottles clinking. She looked fed-up. It was the end of the week.

Want to come in? she gestured with a flap of the dangling shoes.

The door stood open between them, a black gashed stripe in the white wall.

I'm leaving town, Adam blurted.

She lifted her eyebrows, but the line of her mouth did not change. She was still beautiful and it made him desperate. He clawed at words.

Come with me.

Are you crazy?

Maybe.

He held a hand out to her and she looked at it. She was very pale, her eyes dark and big. Her mouth, too, was dark, like she had been drinking blood.

She looked up at him, drunk and pale and forlorn. I can't.

His hand fell on the side of his body, limp.

Goodbye, she said. Stepped into the black stripe. Closed it. The wall was complete and black and white again.

Beyond the Doubting of Shadows

Too many events in a man's life are invisible.
Unknown to others as our dreams — Anne Michaels

Still more remarkable is the fact that our knowledge changes too, some
items emerging, while others are lost — Plato

An emeritus professor of dead languages in the School of Classics, Sophie Ivy Reed knew, but had not realised, that she was like a moth following a beam of light directly to its source. For some years now, there had been something like a huge shadow in her life, a space she had entered step by step, slowly extending herself into the dark. She had dreamed of incarnate gestures in stories she'd written from that place. And when he arrived at the end of summer, she saw that she was scared, or perhaps more excited than scared, though the excitement was toned down by a certain sense of duty.

She had known of his coming, of course. She had thought his decision odd, rash, reckless, even. Who would ditch a successful surfing career at the drop of a hat? On closer inspection – of the act, not the wording – she could understand, for she'd done it herself. But who would choose the country campus of one of Australia's oldest sandstone universities to study poetry and philosophy? That was beyond her understanding. But it was his decision and she had to accept it despite – or perhaps because of – her having been instrumental to it through some fluke of fate.

Professor Sophie I. Reed, author of *A Stardust Audience*, was trying not to dwell on this, the day his flight was expected. At 3:00 pm, she decided to take a short walk and headed for the library. It was a hot day, and the harsh, beating sun came out amid the high branches of the gum trees on the university car park, scorching and spreading out with a flush of chrome green after the recent rain. There were gusts of wind blowing gum blossoms. Sunshine everywhere.

Sophie spotted him from the car park on her way back to the Classics building and felt like calling out his name. But she checked herself as she checked her watch, ashamed of her own impulsiveness. After all, he was only due to land at 3:00 pm. And according to her watch, he was just getting through customs at 3:14 pm. She hurried back to her building and up the stairs to her office.

Confidently, she turned the door handle.

Now that was strange.

There he was in the corner of her right eye, defying the laws of time.

She recognised him intuitively – the way he moved with purpose.

Sophie Reed tried to make herself dislike him. She looked for signs: the arrogant French upbringing cleverly disguised among impeccable manners, the Californian accent, the loudness of his presence in her office, the goatee, the perfectly aligned white teeth, the gorgeous elf ears that were surely pinned back, the pierced earlobes, the tattoo, and above all, the smell of cigarettes that clung to him.

But what she found she actually disliked as she listened to his story was some obscure affinity.

Like herself, he was a nocturnal migrant, crossing from coast to coast, with nothing at the end of his journey but a guiding light to divert him from his course. And this set off distant alarm bells.

Because in their conversations he constantly made references to Plato's arguments and use of metaphor in *The Republic*. Sophie instructed him to read *The Symposium* and write a critique of Socrates' argument with Diotima.

But soon, Sophie would delight when he came whistling past her office. Soon, she would welcome his slipping in unconcealed through the door at any time of day to ask questions and answer just as many; to destroy all that seemed evident and make solitude exhilarating, complete, irrelevant. She would learn that you think by means of synthetic images that follow each other at great speed, landing every now and then on linguistic fields, though never staying there for too long and flying off again to return to a grammatical airport. Soon, she would notice something in his voice, or perhaps in his manner, that spoke of loss. And this would move her. Then she would ask herself who indeed was this guy with a mind the size of a planet and the wild wonder and buried grief of a child.

Soon, after the heat had died down in the evening, she would drive out slowly, listening to *Oasis* all the way through the blue cloudless sky and the light so dazzling. At times, she would have to stop on the side of the freeway and shut her eyes. She would then listen to the noise of traffic and study the map in her heart and conscience. And she would ask herself who would not be grateful for this?

On campus, there is a small agora between the North and South buildings on the far side of the lake. In autumn, Sophie made a habit of going there after the day's work to stop what had become a constant moving back between two lights. Sometimes, she would watch the sunset there so that she would not get lost on the way home. She saw that when the sun was setting behind the hills and the light was falling gently on the stones, the air took the shape of dreams.

One day, as she leaned across the rail from where you could see the hills breaking the sky, she smelled the smoke that hovers about him. He waved at her and before she registered that the hills hung mirrored in their shades like a poem flaunting its metaphor, he was leaning on the rail next to her.

He jerked back and pulled out a packet of cigarettes from his breast pocket, took one and lit it. When he flicked his lighter, she saw an unblinking star, but dismissed the image. Replacing the packet to its home, he lifted his head and looked at her. He took one drag from his cigarette and exhaled, giving her a small nod. He took another puff. She didn't miss the satisfied sigh he let out and watched the grey tendrils pour out of the lit end of the cigarette, reaching out into the space around it like a living thing.

As the cigarette shrunk, she felt a wave of heat rush through her body and a violent desire for one. He scrunched the remnant of the cigarette on the rail and threw the butt into one of the small bins across from the agora. He sat down on the top step of the circular flight of steps and lit two cigarettes. He passed her one as she sat down next to him.

The sun was gone but the evening was warm.

Any moment now he would glow next to her. She dismissed the thought, like a cliché. Then all of a sudden, he turned to her and said, his voice gravelly:

Are you ok SIR?

I thought you'd know.

I don't understand.

It seems we read each other's minds.

And finish off each other's sentences.

True, but absurd.

A total silence came about. Almost strident. Discordant. At the far end of the building on the North side of the agora a light came on. Sophie thought of Rembrandt and of paintings where the scenery would only return light that came through its windows. Light and shadow, thought to be real, yet in reality, ghostly, unreal and oneiric. The conversation could have ended there, but to break the spell she asked:

Where does that light come from?

Badly phrased question. You should ask where do those shadows come from?

A black light, angelic and cold, she said flatly, where the imagination burns through, undazzled and dazzling.

He burst into laughter, taking in the irony. Then more silence, a silence louder than the previous one, only interrupted by the call of an owl somewhere in the distance.

What was that noise?

Wrong again. You ought to say where do these silences come from?

And who do you think you are? Grand Jacques?

I am a question corrector.

It seems you come up with a new job every day.

Fallacious interference. I mean inference.

Anyway, do shadows speak?

No, but their spokespersons do. Which means shadows remain silent, but their silence can be heard.

Well, then, where do those shadows come from?

It depends; some shadows are merely the exact compensation of light, its natural consequence, or its double.

That may be so, but in this kind of scene, right now, the light is beyond the pale.

Why so French?

Pardon?

Well, there are shadows and shadows.

I thought that all shadows belonged to the same half-light or penumbra.

Ooh. Only in the same way that all lights are part of the same blinding light. Light blinds. Shadows show.

Though Sophie Ivy Reed wanted to say she didn't need a philosopher at that point, she did not answer anything to that. She ventured a glance at him and saw that even in this twilight he seemed to be shining. She took a drag from her cigarette and watched the thin bluish smoke she exhaled drift. She could sense him shifting next to her and was aware of the texture of his clothes and of some slight rustle. Soft-rough, like skin needing a shave. She felt the voiceless ending stick in her own throat, so half-closed her eyes.

At that moment a form took shape and shone from the shadows of her childhood. There, in the sun-drenched sand of the Sahara, not the Australian agora or its desert, stood the Little Prince.

Stone Heart

To lose one's life is no great matter; when the time comes I'll have the courage to lose mine — Albert Camus

The name is Man, you wrote. Previously Mandy. You live with Attila, a tomcat who shares your bed. You've never had sex. The thought disgusts you. You don't like this bit, that's okay. You don't have to like it. The beard suits you. It might help you transition. It will look good in court. Trimmed. Let's resume, shall we?

You crouch and duck through the undergrowth, stalk the torchlight up ahead. You stop in your tracks. Your mud-caked pants cling to your shins. The palms of your hands, hot and roughed from crawling through bracken, ache. It's dark, but you can tell by touch your gloves are wrecked. Your legs weigh a ton. Your back is sodden, neck stiff, chin itchy as hell.

Pity there is no moon. You listen for movement in the distance; align yourself towards the sounds of breaking twigs. Rustling on either side means they are following. If you weren't so tired you'd be relieved to know they're stepping into your footsteps from shadow to shadow. Your exact words. You smell them now. A whiff of farts, musk, smoke, caramel, methylated spirits, sandalwood: Prout, Nancy, Excell, Davy, Ark, Leave. The sweet piss of the diabetic: Ollie. All assembled.

Ahead, silhouettes of skeleton trees and she-oaks red from the fire below. The others have lured you back to their camp. You break right, steer your lot into a trench in a dry creek bed. You move faster, back pressed against the vertical bank as you side-step the tall spike-rush. Just as you thought: the peaks of green canvas tents, still and silent under black wattle.

Past the first cluster of tents you are out of bounds. You know that. You peer over the trench wall. The fire, now only twenty metres away, is sentried by a stone man. He reminds you of your father, the unsmiling physician: a rigid and hard block that stops everything and everyone. Your words again. Notice he's already petrified in your account, your father.

Now let's put this bit into the past: My father was a country doctor. He liked and trusted no-one. He never took holidays. Went fishing on Sundays. When pop died he bequeathed a bush block to the Boy Scouts. We all frequented the Wolf Cubs as kids. Taught us bush survival skills and how to tie knots. Overhand knots, half knots, square knots, slip knots, nooses. You like lists. You say *pop*, not *dad*.

Look at me. It's my job to reconstruct your story. I want to bring you right back there. On Anzac Day 2016.

Why?

I ought to have stated my purpose in opening, but surprise is part of our method.

With care, you scale the bank and roll onto the ground. Each of you disappear into the fernery in different directions to begin your individual tasks. You surveyed the place by day, so yours is to take down the flag next to the fire. You aim at a drooping cassinia – I had to look that up – five metres from the fire. You inch along the ground, your arms carrying your body forward and your toes propelling you along the ground, as you've learnt from Davy, the expert at commando crawl who lives in a rabbit hole. Davy's the baby who died, right?

Yes.

Makes sense. *What*, asks the novelist, *makes us want to know the worst?* But we are not writing a novel. Let's get the facts right. I'm nineteen, you stress. And I'm fat, like my father. Interesting identifications. No need to squirm.

The only thing on your side – as long as you remain flat on the ground – is that the fire is recessed in a pit. You crouch-crawl along, obscured by the branches. The sentry, you point out, would only be able to see in the small radius lit by the flames. And you add: as soon as the scrub takes off, he would have no hope of seeing anything in the flickering light. This smells of premeditation. Don't worry, I'm not writing a charge sheet. You've been to court before?

Yep. Shoplifting, graffiti, drink-driving.

For a planner, you don't waste time. I note that no conviction was filed.

(Nod).

You automatically agree, as if the matter isn't worth discussing. As you wish. Let's push on … at the base of the shrub, you plant your knees on the ground. Wait for an opportunity to steal the flag. Sit there huddled while Stone Man snacks and snacks like Nancy, who'd protect the world from boys and boys from the world. Nancy who'd gorge and vomit food, especially strawberry jam sandwiches that would make her teeth red, like a vampire, you say. Nancy who'd cut her wrists and fat stomach. You are not self-harming, are you?

No.

Okay. Stone Man wanders off into the scrub on the other side of the fire pit for more firewood. Looks at his watch. Strides round to a barrel only a metre from you. Sparks a match and sets a bunch of papers alight. Fans the flames. When the fire takes hold, you realise the barrel is a large water boiler like the one Leave tipped over himself the year you last went to Venus Bay as a family.

Mum's okay, you say, when she doesn't have that evil eye of hers. What do you mean by evil eye? Does she have a mean streak? Ah, a bit of a temper. An impulsive woman. You digress from your narrative, but that's fine. It's your job to free-associate: When I was little, I couldn't sleep. I used to imagine cutting myself all over. I'd also picture my father cutting off mum's head, raping me, then cutting his own throat. A disturbing fantasy. And sleep would come?

(…)

Ready to make a run for the flag, something holds you back. Stone Man has resumed his post. Prout joins him. Prout, whose task, duty and mission in life is to destroy any love what is given. Hmm. Curious. We are in allegorical territory. Would you care to elaborate?

Perhaps later.

In need of some inspiration, you draw a foil tube from your webbing and chew on the sludge that squeezes through the plastic nozzle. The taste of strawberries. Fire. Foil. Fun. You twist the nozzle tight. Sling the thing underhand at the base of the boiler. The tube makes a soft thud as it hits the glowing ambers. An Excell act. Neither Stone Man nor Prout glance over.

Pffftkkhhufffff.

Thank you for voicing the chemical explosion effect. Your words. The tube bursts. Jam sprays everywhere, shooting streams of red goo through the trees and down on the ferns and cassinia. The canopy of scrub shields you against ruby droplets hanging in the branches of yellow box overhead. You must love trees. You know their names. You crouch-run through ferns, away from Stone Man and Prout. Freeze. You remove your knife from its belt pouch. Pounce onto the line that holds the flag and cut it with one swipe. You wrap the string around your hand and run. Sucked into the dark. But you are being pursued. Head south-east, with the breeze. There are tawny stripes in your field of vision. You feel like you're melting into the foothills. You twist your head out of this sensation. You crane and listen. An owl swooshes through the tree tops. Crumbling earth and splitting branches make you spin around with a start. A figure drops to the ground and crouches still like a cornered rabbit. You hold your breath.

We are running out of time so, if it's okay, I'll read out your own text back to you now:

What have we here? The figure tenses and looks about to turn and run. Ollie. Of course, he grew stout after he came out and went inward.

Ol, I whisper.

Man?

Where's Excell?

Waiting with Ark and Leave at our rally point.

Let's get cracking.

Of course, Excell would be waiting. Of course, Ark and Leave would be, too. Excell watches them like a hawk. The good doctor drove them both out of home and cut them off. Now Ark cross-dresses, paints and drinks. Leave, who tried to drown himself at fourteen, is neuter. He's got tablets stashed away for later.

The ground, dry up to this point, is getting sludgy underfoot. A smell of soap and rotting meat. Above the rim of the creek, a mobile kitchen. Something catches my shin. I try to kick it off. The snag sticks. Ollie is kicking around. The lights of the kitchen flick on. Light cast out the window shines straight onto us. Rakes the ground. We scamper into the shadow along the bank wall and stand there, tense, pressed against the earth. There is nylon fishing line coiled loose about the place.

Keep going Ol, I say, crouching to scoop up a handful of stones. I'll distract them. Which I do: every ninth step, I turn. Hurl stones at the tree line on the other side of the creek.

Sunlight hits the canopy of gum leaves. Red stringy bark here. Insects buzz on the wind. Magpies call out. A kookaburra cackles. We take a seat on the culvert at the roadside. Excell, Ark and Leave emerge from the trees. Davy trails behind them, tiny and limping. No Prout, of course.

Man!

(I don't know how people cope, watching the world go past from the other side of the mirror as mum does. Man, she'd say, all art is endurance. One day you'll understand. Mum was a poet. Both breasts removed for cancer last year. One of her arms swelled stiff, the other flapped like a useless appendage. They've just amputated it. It weighed a stone.

What does it feel like to be mutilated? I asked.

Man, she chortled, there are many ways of putting a knife to good use. Just think of me as the Mike Parr of poetry.)

Seated on the culvert at the roadside, I feel small. My right wrist is sore. My thumb swells. I try to distract myself from the pain. From the exhaustion. Narrow leaf bitter-pea, sweet bursaria and grey parrot pea grow on the side of the road. Further afield the sparser ground layer gives way to a wealth of orchids and lilies.

The end of your account. Quite poetic …. if you could see the expression in your eyes.

He was a cruel man.

Stone heart?

He'd make fun of mum's infirmity if that's what you call it. Doctor though he was, he took no interest in her illness. Never visited her in hospital.

Nurse her?

I did. I moved into a bedsit close to them so I could look after her.

It's time for you to face the facts.

I hesitated. I …

Let me quote Freud in your defence: *biographical truth is not to be had, and even if it were it couldn't be used.*

I didn't kill him.

Who did?

Prout might have.

Unlikely. In your story Prout, whose task, duty and mission in life is to destroy any love that is given, sticks to your father. He betrays you.

B-but …

By the way *prout* is the French word for wind. As in breaking wind.

Ollie did. I mean da-ad used to call him *shemale*. Back in the Wolf Cubs days.

Ollie. With your knife?

He jammed it in his neck. You saw the coroner's report.

But Man, you know as well as I do that Prout, Nancy, Excell, Davy, Ark, Leave and Ollie are all the same person. *Many in one*, the novelist would say. From the other side of your mother's mirror: you.

Yes.

Thirty-Three Days

The secret to happiness is freedom …
And the secret to freedom is courage. — Thucydides

I saw an ibis today.

An ibis?

I was at the gate and saw it fly over the house. I wind some linguini around my fork. Thom drains his glass of wine. There is pesto in the corner of his mouth. I don't tell him. Pass the water, please. I pour myself a glass. It is icy, hurts my teeth.

In bed I lie on my back and look at the shadows on the ceiling. I think about the ibis. How strange it felt to see one in the city: an elegant white bird high over black streets, black factories, black chimneys. Thom's already asleep. I listen to his breathing. Remember when it used to make me feel safe. Now it grates inside. I take my pillow and head for the lounge.

I'm standing in the backyard when I see it again. Now there is a whole flock of them tearing through clouds towards the creek.

What are you looking at?

You scared me.

What are you looking at?

Look: ibises.

Oh. Thom clips and unclips the plastic pegs on the empty clothesline. Slides them along the wire. How's your sister?

She's fine, I suppose. My eyes scan the pot plants under the verandah. One of the large leaves on the lily is serrated from the work of a caterpillar.

It's hard, Thom says. I know it's hard.

I have my back to him. I feel him watching me, but don't turn around.

Thom is drying the dishes, a smile on his face. I rub my eyes. Sit down at the table. She doesn't even know me, I say.

What do you mean?

She thought I was one of the volunteers.

What the?

I know. I said 'I'm your sister. Dom. Hello.' I wanted to add 'Dominic fix it,' but didn't.

Thom puts down the tea towel and reaches out to touch my cheek. I swing my head around. Get up. Put the dishes away.

I bought a box of scorched almonds, he says. I thought maybe we could eat them later, have a glass of wine before bed.

No, thanks. I think I'll go to bed now.

Go on, just the one.

Just the one, eh? No.

Fresh cotton sheets. Crisp and cool. I want to cry. Once I was the big sister who'd clean up her mess and cover up for her. Now I'm just a stranger.

Even Amy's given up on her, I say as Thom climbs into bed.

That's tough.

That's the thing. Daughters are not supposed to mother their mothers, are they?

I don't know.

I roll over and try to look at Thom in the dark. All I see is a shadowy silhouette. I reach out and touch his face. Briefly. I wonder how much grog you've got to drink to fry your brain. How much pot you've got to smoke. Maybe Thom will wake up one day and not know who I am. Just a stranger lying on the other side of the bed. What would he remember? But I know that's not the real issue.

Promise me, I say.

Not again. You're barking up the wrong tree. There's no fucking mental illness in my family.

Your brother killed himself.

Your sister Pip was anorexic. Is. Plus she used to drink like a fish.

But it's the pot that tipped her over the edge.

Come on. Thom kisses my fingertips, but I take my hand away and lie still.

Pip lies prostrate on a chaise longue in the sunroom, her gaze lost out the window, a copy of *Vogue* at her feet. The tin of shortbreads I brought last week sits on the coffee table, a note propped on the lid: *Help yourself.*

Hi. I brought you some nail polish.

How did you know I love nail polish?

I just knew.

Pip sits up, spreads out her fingers before me. I unscrew the bottle and begin to paint her nails. It's quite hot outside, I say.

This reminds me of gin and tonic. The smell, I mean. It's been so long.

You're doing well.

When I was little, my sister used to paint my nails.

Mmm. You used to paint, too. Pictures.

I was quite artistic.

There's an Art Room here. Perhaps you could …

I don't think I'm up to it. I'd just want to … I don't know. It's so beautiful out there.

Yes, hard to think you're in the city. Anyway, I'd best push on. I stand up.

Thanks for doing my nails. Sorry, but I can't remember your name.

That's okay. We all forget things. I'm terrible with numbers. I'm Dom.

I once knew a Dom. Dominic. 'Fix it, Dominic, Fix it!' Can't remember where that's from.

That night I water the plants and watch the ibises fly towards the creek. I find it difficult to imagine that on the other side of all the concrete and lights and petrol fumes there is a creek. Even the word creek sounds quaint. A place of mud and rocks and dusty green. I wish I could fly, like those white paper aeroplanes drifting in the sky. When the dark falls on the shape of shadows I go inside and hop into bed.

Early night, Thom says.

I'm tired.

I haven't seen much of you lately, he says, climbing in beside me.

A sigh. The air in the room is heavy, warm and sticks to the skin. Thom?

Mmm?

Have you ever wanted to fly?

I guess. When I was a kid.

What about now?

Not really. He inches his way closer to me. Do you?

Sometimes. I can smell his breath. Pull the sheet around my shoulders, close my eyes, then say: it's been thirty-three days.

Kleptorama

Here she is again. Same spot. Same time. She is eating a chocolate bar she bought the night before.

I remember her because she stood out from the other customers. She didn't lean forward on her tiptoes or with her hands behind her back when she browsed. She took a step forward, turned away from me, nonchalantly brushed the display rack and stood in front of the newspaper pile to adjust her pants. She swivelled on her heels and marched back to the chocolate rack. Grabbed a raisin and nut bar and paid with a handful of coins, most of them ten and five cents. I wanted to laugh. Didn't bother counting.

Watching from the corner of my eye, I continue serving her.

Would you like a bag with those?

No thanks. I've got mine. She packs her Coke and Kit Kat in her backpack, taking her time as I turn to the new security monitor in front of me.

Two clicks and camera three is enlarged: the teens I suspect are up to something in full. They don't look older than fifteen. The one with an orange Billabong cap has his back to the camera; the other, Ripcurl beanie pulled down to his eyes, I've seen before. Both have baggy jeans with chains hanging at the side. They are coveting *Ralph* and *Maxim* magazines.

I stride to the back of the shop. Neaten the stack of Sudokus. Rattle a box of tape dispensers.

Need some help?

The lads exchange glances. Amble out of the shop, their hands in their pockets.

Same spot. Same time. She finishes her chocolate bar. Approaches me.

Hi.

You don't remember me, do you?

Nope, I lie.

What did you do about the guys who were trying to steal mags?

I scared them off.

They were so bloody obvious.

How did you know?

She shrugs her shoulders. Crosses the road, backpack on her back, and disappears into the crowd.

Same spot. Same time She is eating a chocolate bar, a paper cup in the other hand. Mid-twenties. A vacant look on her pale face. Lank blond hair. She wears an oversized black jacket over a T-shirt and black slacks, with black lace-up boots. She pockets her wrapper, produces a cigarette from her breast pocket, lights up. She adjusts herself on the bollard, fag in one hand, paper cup in the other. Her nostrils dilate as she breathes out. She looks beautiful in a grungy kind of way. The graffiti on the walls that flank the alley, the chalk drawings on the footpath, the lifting haze enhance her strange appeal. A tap on the back:

I warned you before begging is not allowed.

She looks up. Shrugs her shoulders. Yeah.

Last warning. Next time I'll get you arrested.

She pockets the coins, scrunches up the cup, throws it in the bin and idles away, leaving the off-duty cop non-plussed and possibly fuming.

I follow her up Brunswick Street. Lose her at the set of lights. I keep on walking. Glancing into the Brunswick Street Wine store and into the bookstore. The smell of coffee grips my guts. Mario's crowded, as usual. I turn around. Quicken my step. The sound of an alarm system. I look up: LORE PERFUMERY. Look down.

Here she is, whipping past pedestrians, bikes, cars, her backpack bulging on her back.

Hey! I call.

A skinny girl straight out of *Vogue* steps out from the perfumery. Scans the crowd. Marshals back inside.

I follow her in. Not a whiff of scent or a bouquet of fragrances, but a cloying pong. I feel queasy. Leaning forward on my tiptoes, hands behind my back, I pretend I'm interested in the vials and flasks and bottles and ampoules on display. Fancy names. No price tags. A lot of testers are missing. I pick up a card showcasing *Dzing!* Between the range *Histoire de parfums* and *Acca Kappa*:

Daring and explosive, grungy and modern fragrances brimming with innovation and passion. Taking the traditional artisan skills and fusing with the contemporary and avant-garde, our perfumes capture revolution's spirit – muse to the modern! Our range stands for a new era of artistry. We collaborate with local artists and stay loyal to the standards of high-end traditional craftsmanship.

Can I help you? asks the *Vogue* girl.

Just browsing.

My next shift is a headache and a blur. I stand behind the counter, head obscured by the smokes cabinet that hangs overhead, only aware of the radio humming away.

Any specials with that?

Nah.

Just your pin number and ENTER. Thanks.

In a split second, more money is spent. Stuff consumed at twice the price just for convenience's sake.

I shouldn't jump ahead. Type in the customer's purchase before they reach the counter, only to find someone else at the head of the queue while they remember they forgot to get milk. I void the work I've just done. Wish I had a register with a barcode scanner. Better judgement.

The teens again. Same scenario. The orange Billabong cap has his back to the camera; Ripcurl beanie shuffles through *Ralph* and *Maxim* mags. I call Security.

Same time. Like me, the creature of habit has changed her mind. She is walking out of Piedimontes. Adjusts her pants. Retrieves some items from under her clothes. Shoves them in her backpack. She dashes into the Christmas pop up store two doors down.

From outside the bay window, I see her helping herself to scarves and jewellery. She acts quickly right behind the cash register as the shop assistant swipes a credit card, wraps a purse, pops it in a bag.

I feel like a stalker. Decide to catch the tram home.

As the tram lurches forward, she plonks herself in the seat opposite mine.

Hi! Where's this tram going?

The Preston Depot.

Do you shop at Myer?

Not if I can help it.

I have this gift card. A hundred. Do you want to trade it?

Haven't got a hundred on me.

Ninety. It's for my medication.

Sorry. Not interested.

She looks through the window, sour-faced. Gets up. Picks up her bag. Drops it at the rear exit. Makes conversation with another passenger who dismisses her with a piss off gesture. As the KFC looms on St Georges Road, she backtracks to the rear exit. Gets off.

Four traffic inspectors in their fluoro vests stand to attention. Should I have warned her? Hard to think. I feel bad.

I fish for my MYKI at the next stop. Gone. So is my wallet.

A Whiff of Frankincense

The kingdom of heaven has been subjected to violence, and the violent are taking it by storm — Matthew 11

No wind. No stars. A half-cut moon thrust against the sky. Bodies of trees clustered close to the creek mark the whims of weather and climate change rather than the cycle of seasons. Oppressive heat. A night to match my mood even as I jog along the path, my ears unplugged, alert to the chorus exploding on the rickety bridge where the water is deepest underneath. A body is being fished out. Distraction, prudishness, or is it just fear that takes my eyes off the scene and propels me forward?

I duck under the trees, strands of hair whipping my eyeballs, steps even on dirt dry as a bone. Sweat drips off my eyelashes. Lungs burn. A stitch. I slow down. Wipe the sweat. Catch my breath. *Ring ring* in my back pocket. My hand reaches for the phone. A sharp pain in the neck. A push. I fall sideways in the long dry grass on the edge of the path and he is on top of me, pulling at my hair, twisting the knife.

I want to scream, but no sound comes. I want to run. Vanish.

The knife. He jabs it again and again. Throws it away. Muzzles me with a dirty hand. I want to bite. No leverage. The smell of stale tobacco. A whiff of frankincense. I know him from way back. At twenty-one, a survivor, I have long been prepared for my own execution. What crime must I own up to? Will he rape me or kill me? Or both? I can't breathe. My eyes hurt with the dust.

It will not be simple, it will not be long. He is thrusting himself into me. I stiffen. Float above my body. *It will take little time, it will take all your thought.* He rams inside the body I see sprawled in long grass. I screw my eyes shut. *It will take all your heart, it will take all your breath.* He pants. Releases the grip on the mouth. *I gasp. It will not be simple, it will become your will.*

A black dog appears out of nowhere. Sniffs the air. A high-pitched yelp.

I smell his terror. He springs to his feet and I see the unmatched socks he has sported since I've known him at thirteen: one polka dotted; the other striped. He bashes his way through the bushes. On the caked mud, a glint of the moon.

Floating above my body, I notice the pool of blood. Feel nothing but burning. The other me bites her lip. Licks the blood. Registers the location of her injuries: backside, neck, chest. Perhaps she is sorry now she didn't stop on the bridge.

I will myself to feel nothing. The earth smells of dog shit. My eyes focus on the swollen moon that hangs low in the sky, cut in half.

Help will come with the touch of a hand, a phone call. Words that will put on hold the *real real* of this nightmare. It will come with the hum of an engine: a police car with search lights that will lighten the veil of the night, a wire screen between front and back called cage and, no, no jaws of life. It will come with blaring sirens: an ambulance with a stretcher to be carried from a laneway to the path through thick bushes and then under sparse trees. It will come with the crackle of twigs and the keening of a stranger's dog.

I make lists, not sure whether I anticipate or recollect: trauma box, gauge needles, bandages and saline, syringes, painkillers, tranquilizers, breathing aid. Will there be a throw up bag? I feel dizzy. It all goes black.

In the ambulance, one paramedic sits next to me. Holds my hand. Says: don't move. I disobey, suddenly aware of the circumstances. I check my back pocket for the phone. The paramedic says not to worry. I want to protest, but I can't speak. He smiles. Says: it will turn up. I burst into tears, feel abandoned. Turn my face away. *It will not be simple, it will become your will.* Oxygen cylinder, syringe depository, suction machine, bag resuscitator, storage cabinet, hanging bar. He says: stay awake. But I'm in fuzz, floating away from my body.

When I open my eyes at the hospital, I see a cockroach cross the ceiling. I hear music whispering things over. *Look clap cock clap cock roach clap cock roach cross.* Sigh. But there is no radio. The cup on the bedside table moves closer. It rattles softly, then shakes. Dregs of coffee stir. Am I crazy? I move contrary to the non-existent radio. Try to roll over. But it hurts. *Look clap cock clap cock roach clap cock roach cross.* Sigh.

A knock on the door. I wish I could sit up. Two blue uniforms followed by a white coat enter the room. They look surprised. I guess I'm not a pretty sight. Glad there is no mirror.

Hello, says the white coat. We'd like to ask you a few questions.

I nod. Even that is painful.

Can you tell us your full name and address?

I answer in sign language, asking for pen and paper. My arms weigh a ton.

They exchange glances. The white coat gets out his phone and texts. A nurse (is it a nurse?) barges in with a felt pen and notepad. I try sitting up. The nurse hoists me up. My right armpit hurts like blazes.

In capital letters, I write: Lacresha Elijah. 13 Roma Street, Melbourne. Rip the page and hand it over. A hesitation, then I write: I don't want to go home. I underline don't. That takes ages. A sigh. It hurts my shoulder blades.

Thank you, says the white coat, who passes the notes to one of the blue uniforms. He scribbles something in his notebook.

Why don't you want to go home?

Shrug of shoulders.

Can you tell us what day it is?

No idea.

Do you remember what happened?

No.

Let me put this differently, says the other blue uniform, showing me gory photographs: who did this to you?

Don't know.

You must have an idea.

The nurse intervenes. Says they can't bully the patient, especially now that the knife has been found. She looks me in the eye. I hunch my shoulders. They hurt. I notice that blood has stained the neck of my hospital gown. I cover it with my left hand. My backside aches. I hold my breath. Draw a picture of a hooded youth in a tracksuit. Large feet. No socks. I'm glad I can't draw frankincense.

The nurse gestures towards me, but addresses the white coat. Michael, she may be at risk.

I can't fathom what at risk means. Or don't want to, so I mime a glass and telephone. Water arrives promptly. My telephone is at the police station. I suddenly feel very tired. It's like a play: all exit.

I must have slept for some time because when I wake up a nurse stands next to me with a blood pressure cuff and a thermometer.

She takes my blood pressure and temperature, points to the sandwiches sealed under cling wrap on the bedside table. I'm not hungry. I notice the wheelchair next to the door. The nurse has followed my gaze.

Call me Maggie. We are moving you to the psych ward for your own safety.

As Maggie wheels me out of the room, she tells me they have traced the boy through the knife. My mood darkens. My heartbeat quickens. I wish I could talk.

My injuries have healed. I can move around in my room and watch the world go past from my window. There is the routine of meals and check-ups and medication. They took me off Risperidone, but I am still on Zoloft. Since they told me I am not in jail, I've stopped asking when I'll be discharged.

Maggie has taken kindly to me. She often calls on me during her shifts. Not only to tend to me, as she sometimes does, but to talk to me. I am grateful, but unable to respond. She wants to know why I don't seem to be angry.

Sometimes I think that anger is no solution. Anger is no solution to my predicament. And no solution to this social, sexual, psychical and ecological war leading to total extinction.

Sometimes I just want to believe in hope. White birds in V formation on a clear horizon outside the window beckon. How nice it would be to fly. I get up. Watch them fly towards the creek.

I find it difficult to imagine that on the other side of this concreted cell with a window that doesn't open and a door with no doorknob there is the creek, the trees clustered close, the dogs. Creek: a place of submerged violence and inarticulate matter, rocks, water. Amniotic turmoil and violence.

I think of him in his own concreted cell with a window that doesn't open and a door with no doorknob. Smell his fear, blood and bones, frankincense. In that order. I see the unmatched socks as he bolted. Hear the swoosh of the bushes. See the glint of the moon on the caked mud. There is no anger. Just sadness and despair. Why did I want to protect him?

When the dark falls on the shape of shadows, I climb back into bed. Try to recall what he looked like the first time I saw him, not hooded and begging outside Coles, but kicking a football. All I see is a shadowy silhouette. I roll over. Hope for that chattering voice. It arrives just before midnight with a cup of tea and a CD. For when you go home, she says.

But I don't want to go home, I write on my notepad.

Look, she says, it will sort itself out. She pats my arm.

I've heard that before, so don't bother scribbling anything. I drink the tea. Listen to Maggie. She just got engaged. Shows me the ring. I finger the fresh cotton sheets. Crisp and cool. I want to cry.

Before she goes, she gives me that quick piercing gaze. Squeezes my hand. I thank her for the CD.

It is Benjamin Britten's *The Rape of Lucretia*. I start reading the introductory notes: a chamber opera in two acts based on André Obey's play *Le viol de Lucrèce* … the chorus describes the situation in Rome ruled by the foreigner Tarquinius Superbus on the cusp of a Greek invasion, the city has fallen into chaos. I read further. I've missed that there are two choruses, one male and one female. Tears well. I buzz the night nurse.

Maggie opens the door:

Knew it. You want a listen?

I nod.

I've got this little ghetto blaster tucked away upstairs. For special occasions. You know, New Year's Eve. That kind of thing. I'll go get it.

She comes back, beaming. It's got batteries. No risk.

Maggie slides the CD in. Presses PLAY. Ensconces herself in the padded armchair. I close my eyes. Tears flow, warm rivulets down my cheeks.

Throughout the opera, the male chorus expresses the thoughts of the male protagonists, and the female chorus those of the female characters. The female chorus despairs at the rape and ensuing suicide of Lucretia. The male chorus intone that all pain is given meaning. I feel rage. Am enraged. I want to tell Maggie, but she has slipped out of the room.

The dark has dispersed the room and with it, the *real real*. A hiccup. I retch, toss the sheet from my face and rub away sleep from my eyes. Search across my pillow for the mouthguard I misplaced in my scream. Sweat trickles between my breasts. Down my back. I lie with the sheet pulled over my neck, my empty chest rising and falling. Rising and falling. I, Lacresha, cling to the sheet with tight fists, ready to talk.

Payback

Throb of bugs in the air. Clickety-click of stick insects. The pulse of the night drops with a kite's whistle. Chatter of columbines. Song of curlews. Swell of bats crying, screeching, squawking.

The curtain of light lifts. Lorikeets squabble in the gum trees. I lace up my boots. Red letter day. Twenty years I've waited for this. I wake up the child.

I hate it here.

What is it you hate?

Angry babies crying.

They're bats, not babies.

The child's eyes widen. Will they suck my blood?

Come on, poppet, they eat fruit.

Don't call me poppet.

Sorry, Ella. Now get dressed. I'll fix us some brekkie.

The child licks the Nutella off her fingers. I gather the plates, wash up, make sandwiches for lunch. Fill water bottles. Juggle four apples. Pack.

Okay. Let's do it, I say. But the child who refuses to call me mum sulks. I will coax her with stories.

Wait, she says, my notebook.

Camera?

I thought you said …

You're not allowed to take pictures of the rock art, but you can snap a bat or a snake.

A Rainbow Serpent?

Best be prepared.

We drive off on a blood red track. Rocks hit the car as we swerve to avoid potholes, carcasses, crows.

Slow down.

I take my foot off the accelerator. Better?

She opens her notebook. Feeds me back my own words:

According to Aboriginal belief, ancestral beings created the landforms, plants, animals and people while travelling along Dreaming Tracks at a point out of western time called The Dreamtime. Many rock paintings relate to these ancestors also known as creator figures and Dreamtime spirits. There are hundreds of painting sites in the Kakadu region that encompass a huge stylistic variety and time span – some sites are over twenty thousand years old. Two ancestral beings left their imprint at Ubirr as they travelled the land in the Dreamtime: The Rainbow Serpent and the Cockatoo Lady. At Burrungu, or Nourlangie, The Lightning Man and other ancestral beings shimmer on rock walls and in shelters.

The language sounds so condescending in her mouth. I sigh.

Ubirr. We fan out with the crowd of tourists in shorts and sneakers, T-shirts and baseball caps, past art galleries, and past polychrome paintings with underlying monochrome designs:

crowded palimpsests in shades of ochre, red, burnt sienna, umber. Groups of stick-like figures sweep across the rock face, running, hunting, burying the dead, chasing ghosts.

Dynamic Mimi, I say. The child ignores me.

We pause in front of more recent paintings in graphic x-ray style that show the external and internal parts of the body.

Look, I say, the Cockatoo Lady. Ah! Nardarmbul, the Cockatoo Lady, not with beak and crest, but as the Serpent!

Okay. I know, says the child, ventriloquising my words. It seems the myth of the Cockatoo Lady overlaps with that of the Rainbow Serpent. A case of split personality. She chortles.

Wait, I say. Is this a game?

Give me a break.

Give *me* a break. Anyway, Ngalyod is an avatar of the Rainbow Serpent who created the Dreamtime.

At these words, the child stands to attention. Go on.

I glean information from posters planted along the galleries. And yes, I go on. Unlike the Cockatoo Lady, Ngalyod never changed form. Long ago, Ngalyod cut a deep gash through the escarpment, moved through a ravine that ends at a waterfall and chose that place for a home. A rock shields the entrance.

And?

I'll ask Google.

Gotcha!

Here we are. Today, the Gagudju people still know where the Rainbow Serpent lives; a place called Djuwarr, where water flows along cracks atop a plateau and cascades to the base of a rock face. At the foot of the waterfall is a dark pool surrounded on three sides by cliffs. This is Ngalyod's home, I say, showing her the picture. It won't be on our map.

Why?

It's a sacred place.

You mean secret?

I guess. Look: here.

I can't see.

Here. Ngalyod's hiding in the yams. See? A circle figure I name Uroboros, the serpent that eats its own tail.

As the child peers at the rock face I key in Uroboros on my screen. I was wrong! The image of Uroboros, or Ouroboros, crossing itself into an infinity symbol is a modern idea that harks back to the Egyptians, Google tells me. But it does retain the meaning of endless cycle.

Too many errors of nomination in this story. How easily I make the other mine. Assume the white version of history. Now the child has lost interest.

Let's push on, Ella.

In the main gallery I point out pale figures. Tell her they are probably whites because Aboriginal people used to call them ghosts. I remind myself to check that later.

We follow the signposts past an ancient Aboriginal shelter. Some people have as many as three cameras around their waists or necks. Most ignore the NO PHOTOS signs. iPhones are handy.

I eavesdrop. The paintings gathered here were restored in 1962.

I wasn't even born, says the child.

Neither was I.

And who's this guy with the big, you know …

The Lightning Man, I whisper in her ear. He brings the wet season and controls the lightning storms. We'll see more of him tomorrow at Nourlangie.

The child nods.

A closer look. The Lightning Man is well-endowed, indeed. He is surrounded by sparks, and has stone axes fixed to his head, elbows and knees.

Two Swedish women request a photograph. My hands sweat and shake. Click! The child glances at me accusingly.

I redeem myself with a story she may not have heard:

The Lightning Man came out of the sky riding storm clouds. See? Take a look. He didn't come with a hammer, like Thor, but with stone axes pinned to his head, elbows and knees. He struck the clouds and made thunder. If he caught men and women disobeying the law, he'd hiss and crackle. Sometimes he'd even throw blazing spears at them. He still lives in the sky. He comes out every year in Gunumeleng, the pre-monsoon season, announcing rains the Rainbow Serpent brings. It reminds people not to make spirits angry.

I'm in the way. Step aside for a selfie. Apologise. Look around. The child is gone.

Ella, I whisper. Try not to look conspicuous as I retrace my steps, calling out her name louder and louder. The crowd of tourists is thick. People stare. Whisper. A park ranger grins. Points to a fissure on the rock face I just walked past.

There she is, petrified, her camera trembling in her hands. High up the crack in the rock is a threesome of bats hanging and silent.

Come on, I say. It's Okay.

When's Dad coming?

It may be a while, love. My hand reaches out for hers. She shakes it off.

We follow the trail of artworks, oblivious to time and space. Suddenly we're climbing a steep hill. Flowstone shawls spread under our feet. A whistling kite circles above our heads.

I try explaining the Dreamtime. A worldview, I stammer. It refers to Aboriginal concepts of *time out of time* or *everywhen* during which the land was inhabited by ancestors with supernatural powers. I'm proud of the word *powers* but struggle to convey how the Dreamtime extends to *now* and *happenstance*. I get lost in songlines. My mind is such a predator.

Is this the Bardedjilidji walk? asks a woman.

I nod.

She looks up. Frowns. Any idea how we're going to get down?

Oh, easy, I say, the track loops around the lookout and leads back to the car park.

It doesn't.

I pay for my hubris. Distraction. Carelessness. Cultural cannibalism.

Eyes fog. Legs turn to jelly. Back a river of sweat. Heart a stampede. My breath cascades. Trickles. Stops. Don't look back, I say inside my head. I do.

Layered sandstone outliers crumble under my feet. I crawl to the middle of the outcrop. The Nadab Lookout. The call of the void. The terror. Focus. Remember that Baudelaire was partial to the adjective *vast*.

Wherever you turn, cautiously, there are views across the floodplains eight hundred metres below. I remember the child.

Come, she says, offering a hand.

In my voice, I hear a wee thanks.

Soon the child breaks off and gambols downhill like a wild goat. I, feeling legless, shuffle down mostly on my ass.

Back in Jabiru that night, a dip in the pool.

Come on, poppet, let's get out, I say. Too cold.

No answer. The child towels herself dry. I want to abscond. Walk off my shame, guilt, rage.

As the child showers back at our cabin, I sneak out into the dark. Lie on the gravel path, surrounded by scraggly bushes. Look up at the sky. The Southern Cross is as bright as ever. Venus and Jupiter adorning it.

The light on the porch is off. But the door is unlocked. I let myself in. The child has fallen asleep on the coach, an empty packet of Tim Tams by her hand. I pull the doona over her bare legs, dab some lavender in the crook of her arms and check the fridge. Eggs. That'll do. We have a long drive ahead of us after Nourlangie.

Pine Creek. Not much water in sight. A gold mining town that stumbled into existence when the Overland Telegraph Line uncovered gold in 1870 as men dug holes for posts. The Lazy Lizard Tavern advertises booze along with Pizza and Parma Night. Holy beer, here I come. I order pizza and chips, a pale ale and a lemon squash. The child scrunches up her nose. The beer will see me off to sleep.

Oh, Leichardt, Giles, Simpson. Puny mortals, so much more driven than us, mere tourists in this country. We look for Umbrawarra Gorge, site of a disused tin mine we might never find. We bolt along the unsealed track now trickling into a narrow path with dried up creeks crossing underneath. Hot. Thirsty. Out of range. The car swings hither and thither. Dips. The child takes off her earplugs. Grabs her seatbelt with both hands.

It's okay. A little exploration, I blurt out.

Huh?

A little explore.

The child laughs. She knows from previous travels that I use the term when we're about to get lost. May be lost.

Florence Falls at last, with its deep plunge pool surrounded by black hard rock cliffs the child ascends. We spend the afternoon lazing inside the shallow, bubbling pools of Buley Rockhole, where a stream tumbles down the hill, bouncing between waterholes. The child dives from the edge of the largest rockpool. I commit to memory the names of plants we come across: cycad, grevillea, turkey bush, Kakadu plum and Eucalyptus koolpinensis, resurrection grass.

When's Dad coming?

Look, he might be a while yet, Ella.

A swamp on the way to Bachelor. Not a croaking sound. The ground is dry, parched. As water builds up, frogs and tadpoles will thrive. We see plenty of dragonflies. And, oh! I spot a tiny blue-winged kingfisher dismembering a frog in a gumtree.

Isn't he adorable?

You're so …

On the side of the road, brumbies. Look, I say, they are so beautiful in pied sunlight.

You're *sooo* full of shit.

I can't think of an answer. Promise something special for tomorrow. The child plugs her ears. We drive on. Reach Bachelor where I buy curly pasta, Neapolitan sauce and two Golden Gaytimes.

We settle for the night in silence.

Edging Litchfield National Park, ours is a lonely car on the track. But as none of us was hungry, here we are at break of day.

Look! A surrealist installation: Dali and Magritte with termites.

I hate you so much, says the child.

I don't understand.

You never listen.

Yes, I do.

Dali and Magritte with termites, she sneers, throwing her hands aloft.

I thought you'd like the termite mounds. They are geophysical artworks.

You talk crap. Not listening.

Oh, look, a horseshoe bat. Isn't he cute?

When's Dad coming?

Not sure, to be honest. Plus, we're kind of out of range, I say, pulling the map out of my pocket.

She snorts.

In any case, Ella, I've left my phone in the car.

When I take my eyes off the map, the child is gone.

Notes & Sources

Last Leg: The italicised lines are from William Lilly's *The Woman in the Moone* (1597) taken from Jason Hughes's 2003 book *Learning to Smoke: Tobacco Use in the West,* Chicago: Chicago University Press, p. 44.

Rrose Selavy: Rrose Selavy, which puns on 'Eros c'est la vie', is the name of Marcel Duchamp's alter ego. This story also playfully references some of Duchamp's work.

Dress Rehearsal: The epigraph is taken from Elizabeth Jolley's 1985 *Mr Scobie's Riddle*, Ringwood: Penguin, p. 221.

Apart from instances of reported speech, the italicised phrases are sourced from the following texts: Lennon, J. & McCartney, P. 'She's leaving home', accessed 30th March 2017, available at: https://www.google.com.au/webhp?sourceid=chrome-instant&ion=1&espv=2&ie=UTF-8#q=beatles+she's+leaving+home+lyrics&*

Quotes from Shakespeare are from the 1974 *Complete Works of William Shakespeare*, London: Oxford University Press.

Off Limits: The epigraph is from Milan Kundera's 2002 *Identity,* London: Faber and Faber, p. 23.

The Gleaners: The story takes its cue from a painting by Jean-François Millet as sent up by Sally Swain in her 1988 *Great*

Housewives of Art, London: Grafton. Details of the original painting are as follows:

Artwork: 'Des Glaneuses' (also known as 'Les Glaneuses')
Artist: Jean-François Millet
Dimensions: 84 cm x 1.12 m
Location: Musée d'Orsay
Period: Realism
Created: 1857
Media: Oil paint

Everybody Says I'm a Liar: The epigraph is from Christina Stead's 1940 novel *The Man Who Loved Children* as reproduced in ebook version by Melbourne University, p. 33.

Beyond the Doubting of Shadows: The first epigraph is from Anne Michaels's 1996 novel *Fugitive Pieces,* London: Bloomsbury, p. 141; the second if from Plato's *Republic* as translated with notes and an interpretive essay by Allan Bloom, available at: https://www.brainyquote.com/quotes/thucydides_384481

Stone Heart: The epigraph is sourced from Albert Camus' 1958 *Caligula and Three Other Plays* translated by Stuart Gilbert, New York: Columbia University Press, p. 2.

'What makes us want to know the worst?' is from Julian Barnes' 1984 *Flaubert's Parrot,* London: Picador, p. 126.

'… biographical truth is not to be had, and even if it were it couldn't be used' is from Sigmund Freud's 31 May 1936 letter to Arnold Zweig. See Freud, Sigmund, Ernst L Freud (ed), 1991, *Letters of Sigmund Freud,* trans Tania & James Stern, New York: Dover Publications, p. 430.

The phrase 'Many in one' is taken from the title of Patrick White's 1986 *Memoirs of Many in One*, London: Jonathan Cape.

Thirty-Three Days: The epigraph is taken from the following website: https://www.brainyquote.com/quotes/thucydides_384481

A Whiff of Frankincense: The italicised text is from Adrienne Rich's 'Final Notations', in *The Fact of a Doorframe: Selected Poems 1950-2001*, New York: Norton, p. 191.

TThe epigraph is from *The Jerusalem Bible*, London: Longman, 10:39

Payback: I acknowledge that I have respectfully invoked Indigenous concepts. I am aware that the term 'Dreaming' which conveys an ongoing process is preferred to 'Dreamtime.' However, I chose to use 'Dreamtime' to facilitate the narrator's task of explaining the concept with reference to western conceptions of time and also to highlight her limitations in understanding Indigenous culture – no doubt a projection of my own limitations.

I have drawn on David M Welch's 2015 *Aboriginal Paintings at Ubirr and Nourlangie* [Aboriginal Culture Series No. 11] Coolalinga, Northern Territory.

Acknowledgments

Some of the stories in this collection have been previously published, sometimes in a slightly different form. I am grateful to the editors of the following publications:

Culture Is …: Australian Stories Across Cultures: An Anthology (ed. A-M Smith), Wakefield Press, 2008: 'Rrose Selavy'.

Food, Migration, and Diversity (eds M Lee and A Penn), 2021, Arkansas Press: 'Dress Rehearsal'.

Inscribe, 6, 2012: 'Zapped'.

Live Encounters, 3, 2021: 'Payback'.

Magnificent Obsessions (eds. R Lloyd and J Fornasiero), 2013, Cambridge Scholars: 'Beyond the Doubting of Shadows'.

Meniscus, 5:1, 2017: 'Everybody Says I'm a Liar'.

Overland, 167, 2002: 'Last Leg'.

Psychoanalysis Lacan, 1, 2015: 'Beyond the Doubting of Shadows'.

The story 'Dress Rehearsal' received an honourable mention in the 2018 Desperate Literature Prize. 'Thirty-Three Days' was highly commended in the 2017 Odyssey House Short Story Competition.

Heartfelt thanks to the wonderful women who gave me precious feedback on some of the stories in this book: Eugen Bacon, Julia Prendergast, Christine Hill, Elizabeth Colbert and Susan Weste.

Thank you to Bronwyn Mehan, Olivia Ioanides, Abby Hugman and Camilla Cripps for their editorial input, kindness and professionalism at Spineless Wonders. Thank you finally to Bettina Kaiser for the gorgeous cover.

SPINELESS WONDERS

www.shortaustralianstories.com.au

www.ingramcontent.com/pod-product-compliance
Lightning Source LLC
Chambersburg PA
CBHW030836200726

48285CB00007B/2461